The High Road

The High Road

by
FAITH SHANNON

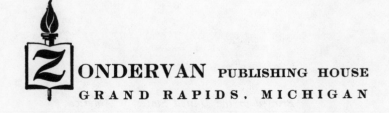

ZONDERVAN PUBLISHING HOUSE
GRAND RAPIDS, MICHIGAN

Library of Congress Catalog Card Number 66-18942

First printing of paperback edition 1970
Second printing   1971

Printed in the United States of America

. . . . this one thing I do, forgetting those things which are behind, and reaching forth unto those things which are before, I press toward the mark for the prize of the high calling of God in Christ Jesus.

Philippians 3:13-14

1

"You should have Anson; he's a riot! The minute he strides into class we all start to grin, don't we, Holly?"

"He's for Lit., Gwen. Brother! If he makes it any easier, I'll take him next semester. Got to minor in something—"

"Why don't you take speech, Liz? That's more your line."

"Just as much work for only two credits, Hol."

"I should think speech would be down your street, Holly. You being from a pastor's family and all."

"No time this fall, Gwen. Schedule full. Boy, what a load! And I'm still wondering whether to teach art or work in an office. I'd love working with children. Liz, what gives?"

"Opening dance, what else? If I can't mend this torn spot I'll have to borrow a formal. Say, Hol, you're just my size. Would you mind?"

Holly jumped from the top bunk and snatched her brush from the vanity. Whacking at her hair-do, she caught the reflection of her flaming face. "My wardrobe is necessarily small. Believe it or not, I have never gone to a dance." She felt the room tighten and waited to hear it burst. Then the tension eased and she began to breathe. These girls were tops. Everyone she had met at State University was friendly.

Gwen's eyes smiled at hers through the mirror. "You're not too old to learn, honey."

"I don't see how I'll manage to find time." Holly dropped into her desk chair and patted her stack of books. "Four stiff courses and my work in the cafeteria every daybreak. Yow!"

"We'll help all we can, Hol." Liz tossed her red organza across the bed and stretched satin clad arms. "It's a bad break when you have to help work your way. My dad is loaded. Two sons in college— that is—my one brother in engineering and Ted, next to me, ready to graduate this spring from here. I'll introduce you two angels to him. He needs someone like you, Gwen, to sober him—or you, Hol, to sweeten him. May the best gal win."

"Doesn't sound rewarding to me." Gwen laughed and looked at Holly. "Shall we enter the race?"

Holly's dark eyes sparkled. "You can have him. I don't want him. He's too old for me!" Her chant brought howls and two pillows sailing.

The noise produced girls from across the hall to join their fun. "Hail to Hadler's Hall. Rah, rah, rah!" The redhead down the hall tripped in with bongo drums and the girls performed the nightly rite of exercises to rhythm.

Holly wrote home to the folks: "Dearest Mom and Dad, Jo Ann and Timmy: I'm just crazy about State U. It's going to be hours of study but the girls are all so nice. Not at all like you thought — they don't make fun of me for not dancing and smoking; they respect my viewpoint."

As the weeks stretched on, Holly did not write that her viewpoint was changing, nor did she mention Ted.

Crossing the campus on a blue and gold October day, Holly ran into the girls.

"We three — roommates — " greeted Gwen, "and never meet outside the dorm. How did this happen?"

"Yes, this calls for a celebration." Liz was a picture from a fashion magazine. Holly admired her tailored coral and brown sweater suit. Pausing beneath a drooping tree which rattled copper penny leaves, Holly tingled with joy. The autumn wind fanned wisps of hair across her eyes.

"Shall we eat something at Renthall's? I'm starved." Holly stepped back to make room for passers-by. A tall fellow strode past as she said "starved." He wheeled with a word, "Liz," at the same moment Liz cried, "Ted!"

Holly smiled at Liz's lightning glance which showed her and Gwen the green light. Her signal fairly screamed, "Here he is, girls; you wanted to meet him; now is your chance."

Ted was good looking. Holly noted Liz's black hair and facial resemblance but his eyes were different from his sister's. He glanced at Gwen, shook hands as he acknowledged the introductions, then looked at Holly. She trembled beneath the long gaze of his dark blue eyes.

"Interesting." Ted smiled at Liz. "You — a black beauty — Gwen, a blond Norse goddess, and Holly — " his pause thrilled her — "a sleek little brown colt. Did I hear you mention the word 'starved'? Let me see. Four bells — two hours till spaghetti and meat balls. What say we four and no more go out to Lazarre's for lunch?"

"Ted, you darling!" Liz leaned close. "We were about to celebrate. We've been so crammed we couldn't get acquainted; all we do is read, read, read — unkink our vertebrae to bongo drums each night — "

"And write, write, write." Gwen laughed good-naturedly. She pinched Holly's arm. Her glance said, "Go ahead, kid. He's fallen for *you.*"

Holly couldn't speak. She moved with the others in a setting of blue and white sky studded with gold leaf stars. Ted's convertible rolled through the campus into city streets like a Cinderella's coach. Holly found herself seated by Ted, with Gwen and Liz in back. Everyone was saying something. Gwen's quip, "Holly's too quiet," aroused her but she couldn't think of a word to contribute. When the car leaped down the expressway, she grew tense. Lazarre's would have drinks. Ted and Liz were accustomed to living high; money was of little consequence.

As they entered the black and bronze bar, she caught Ted's remark, "The guys here know me, Liz. You can have your drink but let me do the ordering and no questions will be asked." Then Holly felt his arm around her.

Was it possible that he really liked her — or had fallen in love at first sight? The mirrored wall pictured a handsome, athletic man close behind a pretty girl in flaming sweater. Was that vivacious face really hers — was it actually she — Holly McRae in an exclusive restaurant with a college senior, the popular Ted Hollister? The new experience was an arch, she mentally quoted, "wherethrough gleams that untraveled world . . . "

Liz steered them to a table by the wall. Holly stumbled in the dim light; Ted gallantly pressed his arm closer and fairly lifted her into the seat. "What would you like, Liz's little friend?" he smiled.

Holly liked his refined manner. Surely his family was one of good background; she knew Liz was O.K. Of course, they were modern and used to the "fast set," as Liz said. But they were charming people to know. Her world had been much too narrow. She found herself yielding her reserve and smiling in response to his expressive eyes.

She was relieved at Liz's tactful suggestion, "Holly comes from a pastor's home, Ted, and isn't accustomed to ordering. Make hers a ginger ale." But she tensed, wondering what his reaction would be.

His sister's words seemed to have a profound impression upon Ted. He turned halfway around in the seat to face Holly. "You *angel*," he breathed. Then he talked with her quietly, ignoring the two opposite them. Where did she come from — what were her plans for the future — he must see more of her. After graduation he was going into business in the next city and would certainly see more of her — now that he had discovered her.

"I've met a lot of girls, but — " Holly didn't need to hear the rest.

While Ted gave their order to the waiter, she felt a new thrill; his handclasp was throbbing with the beat of her own heart.

2

Since Ted was a submerged senior and Holly's schedule kept her in a whirl of activity, their meetings were few. Liz urged Holly to learn a few of the newest dances which were "only contortions to rhythm, and good exercise." She offered Holly a fancy dress she had bought and disliked the same day. Holly knew of the coming party in Chandler House when freshmen would be introduced to upper classmen. She would be there — she couldn't help it, for she was in love. When Ted came gliding to her in his commanding way, she should not disappoint him.

She felt foolish practicing the prances of the newest dance craze, but the girls urged her to learn. "You're a natural at this," Liz told her. "And how will you ever get on in the world if you don't come out of your shell?" Holly twisted and turned to the drums but she didn't feel comfortable. *I'm not exactly sure I want to come out. It all depends — what for?*

Gwen praised her. "I'm too tall to twist around gracefully; you do it just right. Just like a 'sleek little brown colt.'"

Under the spell of their friendliness and the memory of Ted's glowing eyes, Holly attended the Chandler House reception. The music held the same beat as the bongo drums in her dorm; she tromped about with the crowd. Where was Ted? In a jungle-beat whirl, she caught sight of him, bending and swaying with a silver-haired blond. The blond beauty was the talk of the campus. Words drifted through Holly's mind in time to the music.

"She's Irene Schuster — you know — the Lawyer Schuster — a family of distinction and wealth. Money to burn. Irene — a right to be proud — but she knows it."

"She knows it — she knows it — " beat the rhythm. Then Ted slipped past with Irene; they met at an exit. Holly acknowledged the introduction, noting Irene's polite smile and cool glance, a shallow, amused expression. Irene rumpled Ted's black hair teasingly and gurgled,

"Teddy has dorms of girl friends — he's so sweet!"

Holly's heart leaped at Ted's wink over Irene's head. His eyes telegraphed, "I want to be with you." Then they were gone.

An hour passed; Ted did not reappear. Holly remembered that he might be studying for midterms and, growing tired of the smoke-filled rooms, she slipped out.

Under cover of darkness, she fled to her dormitory. "I hope the girls are out late; I want to be alone." Her whisper exhaled like smoke in the frosty night air. It was good clean air. Somehow, she felt depressed.

The dorm was a tomb, a refuge from the whirl at the reception and noisy campus of undergrads. Without turning on lights, Holly mechanically unzipped the frothy gown, changed to her robe and slippers, and crawled into her top bunk. Street lights gave the room a twilight glow. *Ted — Ted — why didn't you come back? Your eyes speak louder than words. Oh, I know you care. I was terribly disappointed. Couldn't you come? Where are you now?* Tears dropped down her nose. Holly sat up. *It's only eleven. I must study.*

She turned on the desk light and looked at the calendar. Three weeks until Thanksgiving. *The folks will expect me home and I want to accept Liz' invitation to their winter lodge. Ted said he would die if I went home . . . he wants to ski . . . I've never had so much fun.* In a frenzy of frustration, Holly slammed her books to one side. *I must write the folks. Can't study. It's no fun at all — not being sure. Why didn't he come back?* Her thoughts smiting her, Holly absent-mindedly began typing. "Dear Mom and Dad: Too tired tonight to study. If the letter is disjointed, it's because my mind is criss-crossed with clattering dishes, bells, books, professors, guys and gals. Ha-ha. Professor Anson is a scream. He makes old novels like *Pride and Prejudice* come to life. We saw the movie — they brought it to one of the auditoriums. You asked if I liked the Arch Street Church, Dad. It's too far away from the U to attend Sunday mornings, but sometimes I get there Sunday nights. They have some college-age young people, but not any from here. Most are away at different schools. Funny — everyone likes to go far from home. I like their minister. Don't worry, I'm working hard but you are working harder to keep me here."

She did not pain them by telling of Professor Anson's jokes about prominent men of church history. Any who happened to have a blot on their otherwise exemplary life were caricatured before the class. The scenes were written in her memory . . . the professor's twinkling eyes and bad-boy expression which captivated his audience . . . his relaxed manner as he paced up and down before the class . . . his words yesterday, "and here is a famous church man — everyone knows

14

his name. But did you know about the girl he met in England — and the little village in France where he sowed his one wild oat?" Everyone in class laughed; some even roared. Holly didn't see any point of amusement, but week after week she learned of more religious leaders of the past who had at one time or another slipped from the narrow path. Biblical patriarchs were not neglected in the professor's list of ludicrous "illustrations."

In science class she was more prepared. She wrote her folks of her experience: "Dad, I had a chance to speak up — in fact, I couldn't possibly have been silent. The prof was lecturing on a phase of the evolution idea and the subject of creation brought someone's question, 'Did the Bible say what we were created to look like?' The prof stood there scratching his head and pondering that he didn't exactly know. Well, I simply couldn't keep still. I said, 'Maybe it doesn't say what we were made to look like; but I can tell you one thing the Bible says which is relative to this subject. God said (I told them the place in Genesis), 'Let us make man in our image, after our likeness . . .' Everyone was quiet a minute. Then one of the fellows laughed right out and said, 'Then He couldn't have been protoplasm or an ape, could He?' Of course, the prof changed the subject immediately. Wow! Are these professors ignorant of the Bible!"

Holly knew that Professor Anson was not ignorant of the Scriptures — that he mentioned Biblical characters in most of his lectures. And that everything he said sounded logical and caused her to seriously question whether the Bible was actually the Word of God or simply a famous book of ancient literature. She did not admit, even to herself, that his humorous, easy manner of speaking appealed to her, and that his arguments sounded reasonable.

She wrote, "I'm hoping to come home for Thanksgiving but would you be able to celebrate without me? The studies are almost beyond me sometimes, and some of the girls have to stay here. I could keep them company." She paused to think of a better excuse and Liz swarmed in with some girls.

"Where have you been hiding?" Liz snapped the overhead light. "I finally got my date to wind up at Chandler, expecting to find you there and here were Ted and Rene Schuster with a pack of friends. And Ted sent you this note. He scribbled it in a hurry. Take it — I'll run down the hall a minute."

Holly opened the paper with trembling fingers. The girls swarmed into the hall, leaving her alone. "Holly, darling. I know you'll forgive me for not coming to you. Rene is an old friend and it's her birthday tomorrow. She made me promise a long time ago to give her my undivided attention for this one evening. Now it will be your turn. I can guess — yours is near Christmas, Holly-mistletoe! Just wait! Ted." Holly looked through the paper. Birthday — tomorrow. Of course that was Sunday; this was Saturday night. But couldn't he have gone with her Sunday night? Sunday made no difference to them. Why didn't the note satisfy her inner longing? It brought little comfort, if any. Irene had him wrapped and tied. Or had she? He had made a promise, hadn't he? A long time ago. And now he would celebrate *her* birthday — oh, no! Two days after Christmas she would be in Dayton with her family. Would he drive a hundred fifty miles to see her? And if he did, what would Dad and Mom say about him? If only she had time to see more of Ted — talk more — discover his beliefs and innermost thoughts. He was grand in manners; surely he must have good principles. His velvet blue eyes seemed to look deeply into hers. *I've met a lot of girls but* — but what, Ted? What did you see in me that you liked so much? You are making me care about you. I am losing my senses. I can't study. What will I do?

Sunday afternoon Ted called her dorm and asked for her. His voice brushed all doubts from her mind and she readily accepted his offer for a date. They doubled with a couple he knew for the concert that evening. She had planned to take a long walk to the Arch Street Church, but a concert was fine; and she couldn't turn him down. His voice shattered her reserve.

They met in the lobby of Hadler's Hall. Holly was assured of his warmth of heart as Ted pulled her arm through his and introduced her to his friends. "Holly McRae, meet another P K, preacher's kid, from Chicago, Gregory Baines. And his fiance, Sheila Strand."

The preacher's kid turned out to be the son of a well-known churchman. Holly remembered her father's censure of his books. Dr. Bruce Baines wrote the "modern viewpoint."

On their way to Lazarre's, after the concert, Sheila bluntly opened a discussion, "Holly, Ted tells us that you are a flying object from outer space which captured him on the first orbit. Says you don't smoke, don't drink, don't play cards, don't dance — "

"Oh, she's improving, Sheila." Ted laughed. "She's learning to dance."

"Take my advice, Holly my dear, and don't start smoking." Gregory's bass voice soothed her nervousness. Holly listened attentively. "I find it impossible to quit the habit and I believe it affects the nervous system."

"Really, Greg. You sound just like a *preacher.*"

"Well, Sheel!" Ted was amused. "After all, honey, you're going to marry a minister. You had better get used to his ecclesiastical lingo."

"With all his study of psychology and homiletics, you'd look for a different approach." Sheila's tone suggested sarcasm.

"There are times," Gregory said emphatically, "that an honest statement, if given a cause, can produce profound effects. I fear that you are not aware of my A's in these subjects you mentioned."

Ted grinned at Holly. "I agree with him about smoking. Once you get into it, there's no way out. Which reminds me — isn't it about time, Holly mistletoe, that I introduce you to something sharper than soft drinks?"

Holly rankled from some of the sarcastic remarks being made. The knowledge that they knew very well what the score was encouraged her to a decision. "I'd rather not. It can become a habit too, you know. And if you went into orbit over me, then you're in *my* galaxy — or something."

Greg threw back his head and laughed. Sheila punched Ted in the back crying, "Hear that. You can't lead this one around by the nose!"

3

Ted swerved into the drive at Lazarre's and spun into a parking place. Holly liked Gregory Baines. He looked more like a football star or a massive opera singer than a ministerial student. He talked to her while Ted argued with Sheila about something. After they were seated, Greg was still talking with her.

Holly learned that he was taking post-grad work at a seminary in the neighboring city. He expected to start his career by assisting a pastor in Chicago. "My church," Greg informed her, "is as large as my father's. Naturally, Pater is pleased. After all my years of hard labor in colleges it would hardly be worth-while to take a small parish. Be a waste of time."

"My dad likes smaller churches. He has had larger ones than the present one at Dayton and the problems were multiplied, he says. I guess the larger the field, the bigger the responsibilities."

"I'm curious, Holly my child. What sort of preaching does your father do, that he has denied you the right to live a normal life?"

"What's wrong with my life? I am a happy, well-adjusted individual. No carbon copy of the masses, but I am contented." Holly's speech evolved from her years of home training. Even as she spoke, she knew that this egotistical young man realized this.

He smiled patronizingly. "Now, my dear, let's not hide behind our religious cant. Throw off this mask of old-fashioned prudery and tell me honestly: you *would* be a happy, well-adjusted girl if you could let yourself *go* and do as you — as you please."

Suddenly Ted, who was beside her, laughed at something Sheila was saying, and leaning over the table, kissed her. Holly frowned. "I'm not at all sure that you're right. Dancing hasn't made me a different person — or any happier — even though everyone seems to think it is such a vital part of life. I don't have to do it to make *my* life complete.

"You see, Greg, your ideas of life and my viewpoint are — well,

18

they are light years apart. Why should you try to change *me,* any more than you expect me to change *you?''*

"You precious, unspoiled girl, I am not trying to change you — as you suggest — I should like to open a door for you. When you once see liberty beyond this open door of self-expression, you will know complete freedom. You will be an emancipated person — your own master — an overcomer of the world."

A smile flickered at the corners of her mouth. A Scripture verse she had memorized in childhood flashed through her mind. *Who is he that overcometh the world, but he that believeth that Jesus is the Son of God.* Aloud, she questioned: "Who is Jesus to you, Greg?"

"Jesus is a great prophet, my dear. One of the greatest — yes, *the* greatest teacher this world will ever know."

"I thought you would say that."

Later that night, Holly, her rest broken, realized that she was reliving the scenes of her date. Something didn't stack up. Ted had spent every minute talking with Sheila. Of course Greg carried on a long discussion with her, but ordinarily Ted would have interjected words, simply to have a part in what was being discussed. He had talked with all three of them on the way back to school; then, alone with her in the hall, Ted had made another date with her and squeezed her hand as he said good-by.

Perhaps it was what she overheard at Lazarre's. That was it. Greg and Sheila, arguing in low tones behind the palms in the foyer, didn't know she was close to them. Ted was paying the bill and soon caught up with her. But she had already heard. Sheila's silky sarcasm. What was it she had said to Greg? Something about his thinking he knew so much about psychology. Then, "So — how far did you get? No-where." His low voice, not so patronizing now, but stern like an irate father.

"Look here. You know absolutely nothing about this science. The way *you* start out repels her — puts her on the defense."

Holly's intuition stabbed through. She sat upright in bed and stared at the window. *Repels her — "says you don't smoke, don't . . ." this or that — puts her on the defense.* Holly listened to a mental play-back of her own voice: *"I'd rather not. It can become a habit too, you know." Yes, Greg was right. Sheila did put me wise to their game. And Greg all but won my confidence when he stood on my side of the discussion by criticizing cigarettes. He did know his psychology.*

So — they are doing their best to make me a disciple for their modern pattern of living. Just as Professor Anson but in another way. And if Ted kept still merely to give Greg the opportunity to preach his sermon on *"freedom"* to me, then Ted was also in on it. Ted wants me to be like all the rest. Why?

She was sure that his first attraction to her stemmed from the fact that she was different from the crowd. *"I have met a lot of girls but — "*

So there. He admires me for being different — yet he wants me to be like the others. How can I be both? I'm all mixed up. Or is he? Oh, that Science exam tomorrow. I've got to sleep.

Holly drifted into a restless dream. Through the following days she drove herself at furious pace, trying to outrun the nagging doubts. Sleep became shallow; she awakened each night trying to figure out what was wrong. If only she and Ted could be alone long enough to talk about life, she was sure that she could show him her side of things. Perhaps after he was graduated there would be more time.

A letter from the folks at home showed their disappointment about her Thanksgiving plans. Her mother suggested, "Why not bring one or two of the girls home with you? We'd make room. Jo Ann could sleep at a girl friend's and Timmy has his sleeping bag. It seems a shame for us to be separated for this family day when you are so close to us."

Holly knew they meant close in heart as well as close in miles. She sighed. "Liz, my mom is hurt if I'm not there for the holiday."

Liz sat before the mirror, deep in cosmetics. "Oh, didn't we tell you? Papa is the same way. Hopelessly antiquated. He wired that he'd bomb the ski lodge if we went up there before Friday. Have to spend the holla-*day* in style. Good old tradition. Aunts, unks, silver platter, and all that rot. Tell you what, Hol. Ted already mentioned that we might angle up your way early Friday morning, pick you up for the big weekend. O.K.?"

"Liz, you darling." Holly impulsively hugged her. Liz scowled. "Made me goof. Does this eyebrow arch to match the other?"

"Oh, I don't know. I can't think. Say, Lizbeth. Should I bring only wool slacks and sweaters, or what?" Holly radiated eagerness.

"Yah," said Gwen from her desk. "Should we bring an evening dress — or big gingham skirt like skiers in Switzerland?"

"That's an idea." Liz sat pondering, her long eyebrow stick poked at one temple. "No — better bring woolens and one good dress. Not formal — just a pretty dress and a pair of heels. We might drive into town for a party or have it there in the main hall. You gals are in for a blast."

"Yeah, that's what I'm thinking. I've only worn skis once or twice."

Gwen smiled at Holly. "You're not the only one. We'll stick together, kid."

"Or fly apart — with the greatest of ease," laughed Holly. "Gwen, could you come home with me? The folks would love it."

"Thanks a lot, Holly, but Liz asked me today when she heard from her dad. I'll go with you next time, if you don't mind. Not Christmas. My aunt has scraped and raked all fall to save my plane fare. She loves me like a mother would. But some other time."

Holly was genuinely happy for the first time in weeks. She looked forward to the holiday with her family; they wouldn't mind her leaving on Friday if she were with them for the family dinner.

On a snowy Saturday afternoon before vacation, Ted asked her for a ride. They were alone for the first time. In sub-conscious thought, Holly felt a crisis near. Ted turned from the highway to a lonely road and straight to a high cut-off which overlooked a frozen glass lake. Surrounded by snowy woods, they had complete privacy.

"I'll leave the motor running to keep us warm." He smiled and took her hands. "Holly, darling, you are a girl who's out of this world. There should be more like you. Unspoiled, sweet, good-tempered — but there aren't any other such creatures, for I've been around."

When he drew her to him gently but firmly, the white snow world faded from view as she closed her eyes.

4

His kiss aroused her from the cloud of unreality. She said breath-lessly, "Ted, we haven't had enough time together. I don't really know you."

He gave a short laugh. "Why do you think I wanted to be alone with you? This is the way to get acquainted, honey. Relax."

She wanted to yield to his compelling arms. She wanted to sink into the oblivion of love. But something pierced through her sub-conscious in warning. Later, she believed it was *Someone* who gave her the power to resist the temptation.

"I'd rather talk more. Do we really love each other? Would we be happy together — as partners?"

Her words restrained him; his hold relaxed. "Little girl, you *are* an angel. You sound like a page from an eighteenth century novel. What shall I do with you? No other girl I've taken out has acted this way. They all try their best to please — but then — marriage *could* be dependent on more than one kind of compatibility. You've got a point there.

"Sweetheart, I'll have to make time to get better acquainted with you. We'll have more dates in the spring term. How about that?" He kissed her cheek, tumbled her hair from her eyes with one hand and wheeled onto the road.

"Couldn't we talk — now?"

"Let's talk as we drive around." He held her hand and drove in silence.

Holly was annoyed by a fragment of Scripture which kept jagging her thoughts. *What fellowship hath righteousness with unrighteousness? and what communion hath light with darkness?* She goaded herself to speak of her personal relationship to Christ but the words would not come out. The way seemed barred. The time would come, she assured herself.

That night she again tossed restlessly. *I should tell him that I'm*

22

connected with God; it is His Spirit within my heart that makes me different from the other girls he has met. He would have the same view of life I do if he belonged to Christ. He would have the same reactions I do, if he accepted God's Word for his standard. Why is it hard for me to show him? He is such a charming person. But he has no consciousness of sin. Is Professor Anson right? Am I clinging to archaic ideas? Does my restricted up-bringing rob me of freedom — a freedom which would deliver me from myself — my inhibitions — and give me a new capacity for enjoying life? A new dimension that others have discovered?

She slept lightly. In a dream, Holly looked through an old-fashioned kaleidoscope of her grandmother's. She saw herself sitting on the ledge of a mountain, feet swinging over the chasm beneath. She stood out from the background in third dimension and looked so real that she shuddered. The depth of the abyss and distance of the mountains beyond added to the illusion of reality. She felt ejected into space as though all earth and matter were insignificant in comparison with her, Holly McRae, and her desire to enjoy life. "It is possible," she murmured, half waking, "that I haven't been living life to the fullest."

Waking, she still had the sensation of standing out from things of time and space. *I haven't thought enough about myself,* she reasoned. *I'm going to that ski lodge to have fun, to get better acquainted with my new friends, and to make up my mind about their way of enjoying life. If letting myself go, as Greg put it, is the answer to my inner longings and frustrations, then, Holly, you're going to go with a capital G!*

The following Wednesday afternoon, when her father picked her up in the family station wagon, Holly had a sensation of leaving familiar surroundings for the unfamiliar. She said, "Dad, it's strange, but I almost hate to leave the campus. I love it here."

His familiar smile and quiet, reassuring voice injected comfort. "I understand, honey. I was in college too, you know."

Along the highway to Dayton, Holly chattered of her subjects, her roommates, and her invitation to the winter ski resort. Her father approved. "We know that you will have an impact on your circle of friends." She glanced quickly at his profile. His eyes crinkled at the corners before a smile broke through. "My, we were proud of you, Holly, about that remark in science class. 'Ye are the salt of the earth,' Jesus said. You help purify every group, every conversation you enter, and help dispense the light of the glorious Gospel of Jesus Christ."

Holly looked at the passing scenery. *If he only knew what an impact they are having on me! If he knew my decision depended upon this weekend up north, he would never let me go. He must not know. I am an adult now, able to decide my own life.*

She said, "Of course I would have had far more fellowship in the Bible College you wanted, but they didn't have my art courses. That brought State U into focus. So — now that I'm here — "

He patted her hand. "God will make you a shining light wherever you go; this is our life prayer for you."

His note of confidence irritated her. She was glad when they drew near Dayton and she could comment on the familiar landmarks. It was good to see the high school where she graduated, the football field, and a few blocks further, the white frame parsonage.

"There's Jo Ann sweeping snow from the steps," she cried. For a moment, Holly was sorry that she wasn't spending all four vacation days right here at home.

Her family's confidence shook Holly. When her mother kissed her and drew back to look into her eyes, Holly's own filled with sudden tears. "It's so good to be home, Moms." After she caught her breath from Timmy's impulsive hug, she sniffed. "Oh, boy, sugar 'n spice 'n everything nice."

"Yeah," said Timmy scornfully. "And you won't even stay for the big ice skating party we planned. They're going skiing too — all your friends from school. Janet Eagan and Carol and Bill and — "

"That's enough, Tim." Their mother touched his shoulder. "Let's make the most of tonight and tomorrow. Holly will be back for a whole week at Christmas vacation, won't you?"

"I'm sure of it. I do want to see the kids. How does Jan like the Bible Institute in Chicago?"

As they visited around the dining room table, Holly felt the close bond of family life. She liked to hear Dad's voice in prayer and Jo Ann's chatter about high school. After dinner her sister played the piano and Timmy followed with his clarinet while Holly helped her mother clear the table. Then the family hurried to dress for prayer meeting. They were having a special Thanksgiving service and Holly knew they would ask her for a testimony. Her pulse raced. She was not prepared. She felt dry somehow. Why wasn't it easy to give a testimony? She used to be prepared with a verse of Scripture any time she was asked.

During the song service she frantically tried to think of what to say. Sitting with Janet and Carol, Holly felt oddly out of place. They sang with gladness which could be felt. Her song came from her mouth but her heart followed a red convertible; she was reading a message in dark eyes which commanded hers to respond; she was thrilling at the thought of seeing Ted Hollister again.

Her reverie was pierced by a trembling voice. The singing had stopped, prayers were in order, and old Mrs. Cedarberg was standing up in front; she was usually the first one to pray. "Dear God, how we do pray for our precious young people. Bless these dear ones in our circle who have come home once again from college. Keep them, dear Lord, in the center of Thy will, a bright and shining testimony for Thee.

"We thank Thee for the testimony of our pastor's daughter, Holly — how she witnessed to those scoffing unbelievers in her science class. Oh, our Father, help her stand firm in the faith and go back in the strength of the Lord her God."

Holly hardly breathed as the quavery voice trailed on and others of the congregation murmured Amens. When her father injected a quiet "Yes, Lord," during the prayer, her eyes stung with bitter tears. Why did she feel so alien here? She seemed aloof, somehow, as though visiting earth from a faraway planet. She knew Mrs. Cedarberg and others who were sure of their faith and sincere in their convictions. But so many of these church folk had never been to college. Of course the Wilsons were an exception; they taught in the high school and were exceptional Christian believers. Janet was the typical Bible school student, living in another world and content to stay in the same groove. Holly did not hear the other prayers; her thoughts were too loud.

When her father asked the young people for testimonies, she found herself saying, "I want to thank you all for your many prayers. I'm sorry that I haven't been able to answer some of your letters but I'm sure you understand. God has been good to me — and — I am happy to be here tonight."

She was happy, she realized, because the atmosphere was charged with love. Every one of the prayer meeting group cared about her and her family; and when any member of the church was ill, the prayer band went to their knees. She remembered the good feeling it gave her long ago when she knew these folk were praying about her broken arm. *They are wonderful people,* Holly said to herself.

As she shook hands after the meeting, she was kissed by elderly ladies and kidded by their menfolk.

"You've sure growed up since I saw ye last," boomed old John Morrison. "Gettin' purtier ever' day, I declare. Comin' to the farm Sattiddy, hain't ye? We're puttin' on the ole feed bag. Kids goin' skating upstate and they come back to our place for beefburgers and ice cream."

Holly smiled and did not explain that she would be away. She wished he wouldn't make it sound so inviting. It was hard to split herself in two, one half desiring the good old times here and the

25

other half living a different life. Old John had personality, as her professor would say. "A unique charm. He gets through to you." What did it matter, after all, that he murdered the Oxford English? People loved the Morrisons because they showed the love of Christ in their daily lives; they were genuinely friendly, and had never been a part of gossip campaigns.

Yes, these folk were real Christians. But were they missing something in life? Were they contented because they had no desire to be anything else?

5

On the walk home, Holly chatted with her family. "It's so good to hear their voices. And it's so good to forget my books. Did I say forget? I have one doozy of a pencil sketch to finish before Monday. And of course the usual book for Lit to wade through. This is the fourth. I think I did all right in the midterms, but we'll have all those books plus more reading for the final exams."

"Jo Ann had loads of homework this year," said her mother. "Timmy is excited over band. I am happy that our family is together as usual for the annual turkey and pumpkin pie."

Conversation was disjointed, each one injecting a phrase or an idea as it came to mind.

"Going to snow and blow tonight," announced Dad, stomping his feet at the door. "How far north do you have to drive Friday, Holly?"

"It's above the lakes. Didn't I describe it to you in a letter? Their modern lodge overlooking the hills — all glassed in — "

"I'll say!" Timmy glowed. "Wish I could go."

"You lucky bum." Jo Ann squeezed her arm. "Rich roommate introduces brother and friends — takes you to their million-dollar ski resort for a whole weekend!"

Holly laughed. "Not really millions. Maybe hundreds of thousands."

"Oil business? Real estate? Banking?" Her father, turning on the lights, looked amused.

"I think it has something to do with a background of wealthy merchants. They moved from Milwaukee and Liz told me her father still owns a department store there. Anyway, money runs in their family. They spend it without the slightest thought. When I think of the way we've always had to manage — "

"It would seem that we are off balance," said her father. "Do they know the Lord? I suppose not, or you would have mentioned it."

"No." Holly took her mother's coat and slid it on a hanger. "But they are simply grand people. So thoughtful and so much fun. I am just waiting for the right chance to tell him — to tell them about Christ and what He does for one's life. You see — Ted — Liz's brother — likes me terribly. He says he's never met anyone like me — and you should see his blond girl friend. She really is in the millionaire bracket."

Her mother seated herself on the piano bench. "Holly, remember that in witnessing, 'now is the day of salvation.' Tomorrow may never come. If this Ted sees the Spirit of Christ in you and falls in love with Him first, he will then be drawn to you and it will be a love that is true."

"Let's eat!" Timmy stomped to the kitchen and they all followed, laughing together.

The phone rang and Holly heard her mother say, "Holly — well, yes, she's right here." Strange, she sounded hesitant. Then her mother's whisper in her ear, "It's Jack. Please — "

A flood of memories colored her face. Holly murmured, "Don't worry, Mums. I'll shake him." So it was Jack again. Jack Martin. "Hello," she said, "oh, just fine . . . yes, I like it a lot . . . you will? When? How nice for you."

"Oh, brother! Why doesn't he dry up?" Timmy's voice entered the conversation and Holly waved him down. Covering the mouthpiece, she formed the words, "Wait a minute — " then said, "Yes, Jack. I understand. Yes. No — I'm afraid I can't. You see, I'm leaving Friday and tomorrow is the only day I'll have with my family . . . well, you can — but — just for a few minutes . . . well, O.K."

"Well, what?" demanded Timmy when she hung up.

"Timothy!" his father's voice sobered him.

Holly laughed shortly. "I couldn't shake him. He's determined to stop by a minute — says he's leaving for Chicago Friday and may never see me again."

"Oh, brother!" Jo Ann echoed her brother's sentiment.

"Holly — "

"I know, Dad. But as you say — sometimes you just can't brush a person aside."

"Sometimes you have to." Mother McRae's face was flushed as she set the table.

"All right. If he doesn't realize by this time, I'll have to intervene."

"I'll be glad if you do, Dad. Give him a few minutes and then come stampeding into the room — all of you."

"What has changed you so much?" Jo Ann looked her surprise. "You weren't anxious to shake him before."

"She's met a rich city slicker," explained Timmy. "He's got her all shook up worse'n the rich small town guy."

The family broke into relieved laughter.

28

"Timmy, you're sharp." Holly pinched his ear. "Yes, folks, Jack said he still felt the same way about me. I said I understood. He said he is going into salesmanship training with Patterson Plate Glass. The prospects are terrific, to hear him tell it."

"That's Jack, all right," said her father. "A born salesman. Not like his brother, Bill, going away to college. But Jack would make a fine Christian. We've prayed for that boy all these years."

"He's a live wire," said Mrs. McRae. "And we'll see what Chicago will do to him."

"Ha!" snorted Jo Ann. "You mean, what he will do to Chicago."

"I suppose you're saving that last piece of cake for *him!*" blurted Timmy.

"All right now — "

"Let him have it, Mom." Holly grinned. "This time Jack will know that I'm out of his orbit, but good."

The family visited around the kitchen table until the doorbell sent Holly to answer. Why was she trembling from weakness? Shook up — Timmy's words echoed in her mind as she opened the door.

She was startled; he seemed taller, his shoulders broader, and more than ever like some famous western actor. He was hard to resist during high school days but she was older now. She had met Ted.

The way Jack looked at her was so different from Ted's look. Jack's eyes held a sadness in their black depths. He didn't rain witty remarks — just stood there holding her hand — trying to say something.

"Won't you come in?" At her invitation he closed the door behind him, keeping her hand in his. "Holly — " he started to speak and seemed to choke. It wasn't like him at all. He had never before seemed uncertain. Suddenly he clasped her shoulders and, bending his head, kissed her softly on the forehead. He looked for a long moment into her eyes and she knew he cared.

"I know I'm going to make good in Chicago, Holly. And I want you to change your mind about me. You're the only one for me; no one else has ever mattered. I'm crazy about you."

"But — you will meet someone else, Jack," she said softly, discarding her prepared speech. "We aren't meant for each other. Our paths are separating. Far apart."

"Please, Holly — write. You've only written once. Just let me know where you are — please?"

"Well, maybe — all right, Jack. But you will change. I know I have in these past weeks. And I can't promise you anything beyond that."

He looked at her with steady eyes, lifted her hand briefly to his lips, then left without another word.

She stood there, staring at the door. How utterly unlike him.

Always he had been gay, even aggressive; not like this.

The family trooped in through the dining el into the living room with Timmy in the lead. He saw her in the hallway. "Don't tell me he's gone already!"

"Yes." Holly dropped into a chair. "Talk about all 'shook up,' Tim." She gave a little laugh. "He's still in love, Dad."

"He'll get over it." Her father picked up the paper. "So he's decided to forget acting as a career. And he didn't want to go on to college like Bill. Well, I hope he won't drift along."

"He will no doubt make good in selling," said Mother. "A boy who graduated with honors in high school has what it takes to make good. Too bad he isn't going on to study."

"If he doesn't let Christ make him a new man, he may go down for the count." Mr. McRae folded his paper. "The selling game requires one's lifeblood. His family, excepting Bill, all live to make money; his oldest brother suffered a heart attack at an early age. Of course he 'lived it up' — as they say. Holly, perk up. He'll meet enough girls in Chicago. And he didn't suggest seeing you tomorrow, did he?"

"No. He seems to realize that I am not responding."

"At last!" cried Jo Ann, "after three years of acting and ardor."

"He sure could act in a play." Timmy stretched on the floor and put his sock feet high on a chair arm. "Was he an actor!"

"I hope he doesn't end up in the wrong crowd," Holly murmured, peering out at the whirling snow.

"End up — " began her mother; then, changing the subject, "let's sing around the piano as we used to, Holly," she said, waving Timmy to his feet and restoring the holiday mood.

30

6

Friday morning, Holly was packed and ready to leave the house at an early hour. Her eyes roved the streets for sight of a red convertible. What would her folks think of Ted and Liz? They couldn't help but like them, but would Ted say the wrong thing? She would hurry them off after the introductions. Mom must not spend any more sleepless nights; she had lost enough rest in days gone by because of Jack Martin.

Jack had told the truth; there had never been anyone else that mattered to him in high school. But there had always been friction between his parents and the parsonage — the Martin's ungodliness and the McRae's Christian life. Jack's mother had nothing to do with the church or Christianity. She was too busy in her social whirl.

Where had she seen that white car before? It was slowing in front of the house. It couldn't be! "Oh, no!" Holly's disappointment escaped her throat. It wasn't Ted's car.

"Who is that in the drive?" called Jo Ann from upstairs. "You said a red car — "

Holly saw a big man climb out and lift dark glasses from his face. Gregory Baines. She shrank from the encounter. What would Dad say if he learned —

"Hello, Greg, what a surprise." She called from the porch. He bowed slightly. "Ah, there you are. We inquired at the gas station. Ted had a load and Dayton was not far from Manton where my friend, Marsh, lives." He turned to the car. "Want to freshen up a bit?"

She heard Sheila's strident voice, "Let's get on with it." Greg bent his head to talk with those in the rear. "Sure thing," he said. "The McRaes will be happy to accommodate." He looked up at Holly. "We'll come in for a minute, if you don't mind. Marsh and Bev would like a brief rest stop. Better stop here than on the super highway."

31

Holly's father came around the house with Timmy trailing a snow shovel.

"Pastor McRae, I believe." Greg stepped forward before Holly could speak. "This is a wonderful privilege, I'm sure."

Oh, fine, thought Holly, stepping back into the warmth of the hallway. *A privilege to meet the man who — and I quote — "has denied you the right to live a normal life." More of his psychological approach. Big stuff. Ted needn't have sent someone else. I think I'll stay home.*

There was Sheila following another couple up the walk. Holly's face burned. Sheila — ugly orange lipstick — and her eyes made up too heavy for daylight. That broad sneer put the finishing touches to the picture of insolence. Of course Sheila would be burned up at having to pick up a nobody like Holly McRae in Dayton — a dump compared to her Chicago suburb.

"Well, hello, this is a surprise." Behind her smiles, Holly felt the hypocrite she had mentally labeled Greg. The group tromped in, removing boots and remarking on the weather.

Holly felt the tension as her mother met and appraised the four. The one called Marsh snuffed out his cigarette and ground it under his heel as he came up the front walk. Timmy brought up the rear, his mouth half open in astonishment. Holly's throat was tight. This was not the picture she had foreseen with Ted, Liz, and Gwen all friendly and well-groomed. Sheila always looked cheap. Her manner was obnoxious. Holly sensed her disapproval of the parsonage.

"Upstairs to your left. Jo Ann will show you," her mother was saying to Bev. She looked at Holly. "I'll heat the coffee. Wouldn't you all like a sandwich before you leave?"

"My dear Mrs. McRae," Greg's big smile illumined his face as he spoke. "You are too kind. Such a hospitable minister's wife is like a rare flower. You truly grace the manse, as my father says to his wife. Mrs. Baines is my step-mother; she has lived with us for some years. Yes, yes. I presume, Pastor, that you have read Pater's latest book *Brotherhood Our Banner.*"

"I'll help Mother," Holly said to Sheila, noticing her father's expression. She avoided his eye and fled to the kitchen. "Mom, they aren't like Ted and Lizabeth. I'm so disappointed. They aren't at all like them."

Her mother looked at her steadily. "Holly, they are all from the same mold. Birds of a feather — and I was worried about a boy like Jack." Her eyes mirrored her anxiety.

"Moms, I can't help it. They aren't like my friends at school. Ted introduced me only casually — and here they are. Sheila is one I can't stand!"

Timmy sauntered in, contempt captured in his eyes. Holly felt the chill of their reactions. Jo Ann running into the kitchen whispered, "That girl Bev glanced around the bathroom as though she had never seen one before. Did you see her fur jacket? Must be real. Want some help, Mom?"

Holly strained her ears to catch the conversation from the living room. Oh, why did this have to happen? Now her folks would start to worry about her and she was getting along perfectly all right.

"Take this tray to the coffee table, dear." Holly accepted the tray from her mother, avoiding Jo Ann's eyes. As she entered the dining el she heard Greg's deep voice.

"This 'new birth' you take literally, Pastor. It signifies, shall we say, the rebuilding of a man. Take a drunkard, for instance. Give him a new environment, remove the old temptations, and you can see the re-creation of the man."

"Perhaps — temporarily." Her father thumbed through his Bible. "Environment was perfect for Adam, wasn't it? Yet he disobeyed God, which act of rebellion was sin."

Sheila stood in the hall door, vainly telegraphing negatives to Greg with her eyes. Holly saw that Greg was engrossed. Sheila muttered an oath, spun on her heel, and marched upstairs to join Bev. Marsh, a tall thin man, stood at the fireplace, hands in pockets, feet wide apart, a sardonic smile reflecting his opinion.

Gregory's bland smile thinly veiled derision. "I cannot accept your theology, sir. Sin. Judgment. Next, you will speak of a sacrifice for sin. You see, I know all the answers. No, Pastor McRae. The only rational outlook as we view the world today is to consider the nations, the peoples of the world, as our brothers. We all have one father, the Creator — if, indeed, the world of men was created — " he turned to smile knowingly at his friend. Marsh narrowed one eye, the smile curving into a sneer.

Holly arranged the coffee table slowly, that she might listen. Jo Ann and her mother were moving about the dining el, arranging things. She knew they were aware of the situation.

Pastor McRae spoke quietly. "If God is the Father of those who do not believe on Him, why do they not act like Him? The Bible says that if any man have not the Spirit of Christ, he is none of His. Those who receive Christ as Lord and Saviour receive His Spirit and show forth His life. 'The fruit of the Spirit is love, joy, peace, longsuffering, gentleness, goodness, faith, meekness, and self-control.' Does the world of ungodly men possess these characteristics of the family of God? The world hates a meek person. And Jesus spoke the truth when He accused even the religious folk: 'Ye are of your father, the devil, and the lusts of your father ye will do.' I am quoting the gospel of John, chapter eight."

"Oh, come now, Reverend." Marsh perched on the piano bench, folding his long legs and shrugging his shoulders. "You don't mean to tell me that the folk in your church are all full of this marvelous prescription — love . . . meekness . . . all that Christ-like syrup. Turning the other cheek — I've seen too many church members. They are no different from anyone else. It all sounds nice from the pulpit but —"

"Look here, young man." Holly admired her father's patience and kind manner. "I fully agree with you. We have few Christ-like Christians in the church; most people are merely church members — some are even hypocrites. Christ spoke of their coming judgment. But remember, there *are* a few believers in this old world who not only have received Christ, but allow His Spirit to control their lives. I have met some of them, praise God."

"But, my good man," Greg persisted, "let's not speak of believers in connection with good —"

"That's right." Sheila moved in, with Bev at her side. "Let's get this show on the road. O.K.?" Her imperious tone commanded Greg's attention.

Gregory laughed apologetically and pulled himself from his chair. Marsh joined Bev and leaned his arms on her shoulders.

"Well, Pastor —"

"Let's have a cup of coffee before you leave." Mr. McRae stood, Bible in hand. "And we shall pause a moment to give thanks. Father, we are eternally grateful for Thy great love. We're so unworthy. Watch over these young people — and our daughter, Holly, as they drive on the icy roads, that they may safely reach their destination. We thank Thee for the refreshment we are about to receive, in the precious Name of Thy Son, the Lord Jesus."

Holly caught the look passed between the two girls. Marsh seemed ill at ease for the first time in their home, and Gregory subdued. They all chatted of school, the ski lodge, and finally it was over. Holly ran into the kitchen to say good-by to Timmy. Her father followed; she turned to kiss him.

"Holly, my girl, you are in the wrong crowd."

"I told Mother," she whispered, "they aren't like Ted and Liz and Gwen. They aren't the same kind."

"Oh, yes, they are. Basically, they are unbelievers. You know that as well as I. What can you possibly have in common for this weekend trip? Stay with us, girl."

"You don't understand, Dad." Holly clutched his arm. "Liz — Ted — would be terribly disappointed. He's — they're counting on me to come. And I want to go."

34

"One word." He held her hands. "Let me remind you of your Lord's warning: 'Beware of those . . . in sheep's clothing' – He spoke of religious people here – and inwardly they are 'ravening wolves.' Holly, I wish you had never gone to this University."

Holly heard the car motor. She cried, "Don't *worry,* Daddy. I know all that. I can't always live a sheltered life."

"I'll pray that you will be sheltered – in *Him.*"

Her father's words skimmed over her head as she bolted from the door. A roar of the motor, a slam of the door, and she was gone.

7

"Do we have to pick up anyone else?" Sheila lighted a cigarette and turned to look at the three in the back seat. "Your lucky star handed you this ticket, McRae. We seniors rarely associate with freshmen; you and Gwen get invited to the hide-out in the hills solely on the merit of your older roommate. I personally don't see this rule — teaming Juniors and Seniors with sophs and frosh. Don't mix after hours."

Holly caught the implication and felt isolated. She was the oddball here, traveling with two couples. Marsh practically held Bev in his lap, leaving half the seat for her. Through the rear view mirror, Holly saw Gregory's forehead crease in a frown. His dark glasses hid his eyes but his gloved fingers on the wheel moved nervously.

"Sheila," he said, "I'm afraid I shall have to reprimand you for your performance at Pastor McRae's. A future minister's wife must learn to use tact in any sort of distasteful situation. I was in the midst of an intriguing discussion and you advanced aggressively like a — a — "

"And I am tired of your long-winded platitudes. We'd have been there yet, if I hadn't used tact to release you from the niceties of a social obligation," Sheila rasped, her face reddening under the orange make-up. "And if you don't get the point, some obligations stick you like this one of Liz'."

"Sheila!" Greg glanced at Holly through the mirror.

Holly caught her breath and gasped, "I didn't ask you to stop by for me. Liz assured me that — "

"Don't pay any attention to Sheel," laughed Marsh. "When she's mad, she's horrid."

"Liz knows her etiquette morals," Sheila flung back. She flicked ashes into the tray. "And I'm getting sick and tired of your cloak of righteousness, Gregory Baines. Always correcting me on behavior as though I didn't have the culture to which you have been accustomed.

36

My father prints your dad's books and was in business long before the great Baines was ever discovered. His personal friends are the financial backers of your dad's church. And you speak to me from *your* lofty pedestal!"

Gregory's forehead cleared. "I am not quite certain that you are going to enjoy the role of pastor's wife. It's not too late to back out, you know. Half a year to June."

"You make me sick!" Sheila crushed her cigarette in the tray and faced him wrathfully. "What do you want — a religious sweet pie-eyed woman — or a woman of the world like your new mother with the know-how in social gatherings? Your father made *his* choice."

Gregory's neck reddened and he raised his voice. "All right, Sheila. That will do. And if this is a sample of our future relationship, I want no more of it. I've never heard the Pater arguing with Lila. She is, at least, refined."

"That's what you think." Sheila's tone oiled over. "You should see her in a card game. My mother could fill you in on the particulars."

"Now, now, children," Bev cajoled from the rear. "Let's patch up our quarrel and unruffle our feathers. See how nice it is to be on speaking terms." She threw herself back upon Marsh while Holly moved uncomfortably.

This was not the thrilling ride she had anticipated; it was a night-mare of unreality. She saw the moving landscape through a mist. Her throat ached from unshed tears. Ted would have made the trip perfect. He and Liz were not of the "new rich" like this brazen girl. They showed good breeding and were reared in a family which had inherited wealth for generations; their pride, if they had this kind, was carefully brushed and stored away, only to be used upon intense provo-cation. But Sheila's spiteful remark cut deep. Was it possible that Liz had asked her from a sense of duty alone? She couldn't believe it. Ted was the one who had urged her to come. She was sure he meant *his* invitation. His last words were indelibly marked in her mind. "Don't disappoint me, Holly angel. I want you there." This im-perious girl would see Ted's interest and take notice. Her assurance of the Hollister's sincerity kept Holly quiet.

Hour after hour passed in the murky car. Greg's blandness finally overcame his anger; for many miles he whistled or sang opera tunes. Sheila smoked incessantly; her exhaling mingled with that of Marsh's saturated the car and kept Holly's eyes smarting. She could hardly wait until they reached the lodge. The thick air was charged with sparks from Sheila's eyes; if Greg should touch it off, the explosion would be something to witness.

Bev tried to mollify the hurt. She confided to Holly, "They've broken up more than once. You can see why." Holly found it impossible to return this gesture of friendliness. As they came in sight of their destination, she let the tears overflow. While the others exclaimed over the brown object high on the hillside, she blew her nose and powdered her face. They saw the lodge above them — a building of modern architecture in several V-shapes of glass, held together with brown wood frames. A sign, *Hollister's Hide-out,* turned them from the highway and sent them climbing a steep gravel road. It was late afternoon when they ascended the hills; the snow had stopped blowing and a burnt-orange sun toasted the marshmallow hills to a golden crust. With relief in sight, Holly thrilled to the magic of the evening. This stifling car of smoke would soon be a discordant interlude of the dim past.

Marsh and Bev went into raptures over the view and the lodge, even Sheila smiled and exclaimed with eagerness. Holly noted Greg's silence and wondered. The lodge, in close-up, made a much larger photograph than the view from the highway. Ted's red convertible and three long, shiny cars were lined up beneath a car port. Greg pulled in alongside and shouts of greeting met them.

Holly was quickly gathering her gloves, purse and scarf, when Gregory hurried around to open her door. He opened the rear door first; Sheila leaped from the front seat and slammed her door, eyes blazing. "That *does* it, Gregory. Here's your precious heirloom." She flung a ring at his feet and wheeled into the doorway as Liz flew out to welcome her.

Holly's distress was acute. Gregory removed his dark glasses and stood beside her; his face registered deep concern. He took her hands. "I can't tell you how sorry I am for her rudeness."

She brushed at the tears on her cheeks. "I'm sorry to be the cause — "

"No, dear." Greg's voice, quiet but emphatic, soothed her mind. "Not because of you. You must not allow this little incident to distress you further. Sheila has become increasingly belligerent the past year. I believe she is emotionally insecure because of a resentment; perhaps she is unable to adjust herself to the prospect of the ministry as a career. It is just as well to discover the cause now and let the festering boil run over. Come, Holly. Allow me to — "

"Holly, honey!" Liz's welcome was warm. She kissed Holly on both cheeks and drew her through the door into a wide hall. A girl in tight slacks came alongside. Liz said, "Holly, meet my cousin, Chrissy. You and Chris share the same stateroom on this ship. She's a high school senior and as yet unattached."

Holly glanced over her shoulder to see Gregory bending to recover his ring. She heard Bev say, "Where's your brother, Liz?" and Liz' answer, "Ted? Oh, he's been skiing with the fellows. Rene Schuster is furious. Nothing going on in the lodge so far, but we'll get things started tonight, don't worry."

"Yeah," boomed Chris, patting Holly's arm and lifting her case from her hand. "We're having a big fire in the round room. I'll show you around. See that circular stair? You can see the main floor from every landing up here. And the bedrooms — that's a laugh. They're slot machines for bunks. A narrow passage just big enough for a foam rubber pad mattress. An overhead bunk makes us a cozy galley. Liz said you were used to the top bunk at school, and I had better park below; you can see why."

Holly smiled at the large girl. She could see no place to hang her dress and wondered at the lack of privacy. The circular wall was lined with open bunks; each was furnished with foam mattress pad and wool blankets piled high. The bunks faced the circular hall and looked over snowy hills from the plate glass side walls. "Wow!" she said, attempting to be lighthearted. "In full moon the light would keep us awake."

"Not me, baby." Chris stood with hands on hips. "After tobogganing and eating the kind of grub Hollisters put out here, I snore like a hibernating bear. Let's take your things to the rest room. They have a closet for your clothes — one whole side of the wall in there. The only drawback is — when there's a crowd — everyone's in a tizzy to use the mirrors and there's only four wash bowls."

Holly followed around the circular hall to a black wood slab marked LIZ in aluminum letters. Chris said, "In the north hall it's TED — the gent's room. Their dad's idea. Cute?"

"It surely is." Holly felt dead and wished she could come alive. A sudden overwhelming loneliness engulfed her and she fought the tears that threatened to show.

8

The sight of Sheila brushing her hair at the mirrors tightened the tension in Holly's mind. Gwen, washing her face, shouted, "Holly, my sweet! Isn't this super? Have you seen around the lodge?"

Holly responded to the warm welcome with spirit. "I'd like to, now that I'm here."

Sheila speared lipstick at her mouth. "She made it, all right. Has a way with men. Watch it, Gwen; she's after a rich husband and knows how to turn on the waterworks or the charm — whichever it takes."

Holly faced Sheila in amazement, then exploded: "Dad always said people judge others by what they are themselves. So it must be you who's after a rich man. You needn't put me in that class."

Sheila's shrill laugh cut in.

Gwen walked over to Holly and patted her shoulder. "Don't take her so literally, hon. Her bark deceives one. I must run. Liz found me a boy friend and he wants to go sledding before dinner. Oh, hi there, Bev. Isn't this tops?"

"Neat," said Bev, looking around. "This rack is where we hang our ball gowns? And look at that wall full of drawers. How dreamy. Which one's mine?"

"Oh, take one. Liz said help yourself." Gwen waved a hand and left the room.

Holly quickly put her things away, deposited her suitcase with others along the rack and was relieved when Chris suggested a tour of the premises. *When would Ted appear? Would Irene be in evidence this time?* Even as she wondered, Holly descended the circular staircase and saw Irene stretched on a luxurious turquoise couch before the great fireplace. She made a striking picture — black velvet slack suit with turquoise scarf looped at her throat, her silver-white hair looking freshly set. She must have planned her color scheme to match the lodge living room. Two young men lounged on the white fur rug at

40

her feet, one holding her hand, obviously adoring her with his eyes.

An older woman looked through a cut-out in the wall and Chris called, "Aunt Midge! What's cooking back there?" Gripping Holly's wrist she said, "C-mon, baby. I'll take you through the main office – the slave's galley."

Instead of a doorway, Holly saw a circular wall. They slipped behind and in a few steps were in a brightly lighted kitchen. A handsome Negro couple in white chef's caps worked together. The chef carved a pink ham; his wife turned chicken over a grill. Aunt Midge evidently supervised; she was tossing a salad. Holly recognized the well-ordered household of the Hollister's and knew that she was indeed privileged to be an invited guest.

If only Ted would come. He surely would come back soon. The sun was gone and twilight orchid tinted the snowy slopes. One wall of the kitchen was plate glass. As she looked across the lighted sloping terrace, Holly saw the skiers toiling uphill. The one without a hood was Ted, his black curly hair glistening with snow. She laughed aloud. "Ted's had a tumble in the snow."

Aunt Midge snorted. "He'll have earache again. I'll box his ears if he doesn't learn to wear a cap. Been out all afternoon, too."

The skiers disappeared in a room below their level. Chris led Holly back to the comfortable living room where they found two lounging chairs. The couches and stools were already occupied. Some were looking at the news; two were at the piano plunking out strains of the newest hit song.

Holly was short of breath. She knew her face must match her scarlet sweater, for she was in high excitement over Ted's arrival. Any minute now he would come dashing in. Gwen came to her with a tall, blond viking named Nels. He was handsome, but his eyes were too bold. He seemed to hold Gwen in a sort of enchantment, for she kept her eyes on his even as she introduced him. Glancing around the room, Holly noted the couples. The two fellows with Irene Schuster now had two girls hanging over them. It seemed that Rene attracted like a magnet.

Someone shouted, "Here's Greg!" The two at the piano scooted from the bench and waved him to be seated. Holly was amazed; she hadn't known he was a musician. How could such big fingers glide over the keys so skillfully? She was thrilled at the way he played. Notes trilled in ecstatic soft rhythm. He broke into a current hit song and everyone sang. Two fellows brought instruments and added the brass for an orchestra. The room revolved in rhythm which captured and held everyone's attention. Holly saw Ted enter from the back stair and followed his eyes to Rene.

Rene stood languidly to her feet before the rosy glow of the fire and writhed like a coiled serpent to the rhythm. Slowly she advanced toward Ted, arms outstretched. He seemed fascinated; he took her hands and began to sway in the current.

Fellows met girls in the strange rhythm dance, moving to Greg's punctuated beat.

Holly caught Sheila's glance which spoke as plainly as words: *You simpleton.*

A kettle banged in the kitchen, the chef called, "Dinnah is served," the music thumped to a finale, and the crowd moved to a long table set cafeteria style. Holly saw Ted lean over Irene. Their kiss froze her smile and she followed Chris automatically. Taking a tray, she glanced over her shoulder. Rene was playing the spoiled child; she curled up on the divan and Ted laughingly joined the ranks for trays. So he would wait on her. Couldn't he see through her type?

Chris voiced her opinion by whispering, "Get a load of that poor little rich girl. Can't turn a finger to help herself. You'd think Ted would see through her, but is she loaded! So rich it's pitiful. Guess she's used to being waited on. He'll have a fine time pacifying her for the rest of his life."

For the rest of his life. For the rest of his life. The premonition grew stronger. Ted and Rene. His cousin, Chris, ought to know. She ought to know. And there was Sheila behind her, smirking. Then Ted saw her and cried above the clatter, "Holly, angel!" He came in swift strides and clasped her about the shoulders, peering closely into her face. "You darling! I'm so glad you have come. I told Dad about you and he wants to meet you some day. Only wish he were here this weekend. Oh, hi, Sheila. Mind if I get in line here? Have to go through twice, you know."

He kept one hand on her shoulder but, somehow, Holly wasn't thrilled. Mentally she decided, "It finally gets through to me that he is nice to a lot of girls. Oh, you dope. Stuck here for the weekend with this crowd. They brought Chris just for you, Holly *angel.*" But she was glad Ted had noticed her while Sheila was watching.

Laughter and talking covered the clatter of knives and forks. Small tables appeared by the walls. Holly and Chris, finding the tables occupied, perched on a lower stair overlooking the oval of firelight. From the shadows, Holly witnessed the cozy scene at the turquoise divan. Several couples crowded around Rene and Ted. Gwen and Nels sat with Bev and Marsh. From the clatter and chatter, Sheila's loud voice demanded attention. She stood with tray poised in one hand.

"Now, now, folks," she called, clanking a fork on her cup. "We must remember our manners. We have here a preacher's daughter and a preacher's son. Shouldn't we ask one or both of them to say a blessing over the food?"

In the slight lull which followed, Gregory moved to the piano, and bending over, struck the chords of the Doxology. Sheila chanted the words, "Praise God from whom all blessings flow." Amused laughter covered the gap and the incident was closed. Her show of irreverence made Holly recoil. This display of darkness brought more sharply into focus the light she knew in Christ the Lord. *What communion hath light with darkness . . .*

Chris plunked her arm. "Why so still, mousey? You sure don't eat much. Say, I gotta see Aunt Midge about going into town tomorrow. See ya."

As Chris waddled away, Holly was again lost in thought. Her cheeks burned at the knowledge of how things stood. Ted looked at Rene with the same adoring eyes he had shown her; she was paired with his high school cousin for the weekend. And Sheila, acquainted with the ways of the world, had seen through the polite invitation of Liz. Holly's mouth went dry and a piece of tender biscuit stuck in her throat. A longing for home swept her like a rush of wind. Since she had no money to pay bus fare, she was stuck for two more days with no privacy, no room to shut herself in. Why hadn't she seen it before? It took a cat with claws to rake up reality. She had basked in a rosy glow of illusion. Of course. She could see it now. She had not responded to Ted in the car that day. If she had been able to sweep him off his feet, she might have had him. Was that love? To scrap over the attentions of a boy? To constantly keep his mind from lingering on another girl? *If love has to come that way, I don't want it.*

A deep voice startled her. "May I?" Greg held his tray, looking down at her. She looked up with misty eyes and gasped, "Oh, Greg. Yes, do sit down." Suddenly she was comforted. He sat quietly beside her, arranging his tray and coffee cup on the step above. They watched the colorful scene and the firelight glow.

"You know, my dear," he said, "I have had a rare experience this afternoon. Your father's sincerity has seeped through and touched a spot in my heart which — well — I am at a loss for words. I — I cannot describe the feeling I've had ever since — "

"Well, what d'ya know!" Sheila's shrill tone silenced him. "Look, Liz. Aren't they the handsome couple? The short and petite sweet and the tall and wide go together nicely. Congratulations, my ex-fiance. You have made a nice little choice; she'll know how to pray with your parishioners."

Greg stood to his feet, dinner napkin dangling from one arm. He did not seem to see Liz; he faced Sheila coldly. "Madam, you are becoming not only a problem to me, but a problem to yourself as well. I fear you are suffering — mentally — "

43

"Call me a mental case!" Sheila's voice rose to high pitch. Everyone stopped to look. Someone's comment, "She sure acts like one," reached their ears and Sheila's wrath blazed. She flung her coffee cup and raced up the stairs, tearing at Holly's hair as she passed. Greg caught Holly's tray before it slid from her lap. Hot coffee covered his shirt front.

"You'll get burned," Holly cried.

"I already have been," he said calmly, his face pale.

9

Liz, the perfect hostess, followed Sheila and did not return with her for some time. Gregory was summoned to the piano and everyone asked to sit around the fireplace while they sang old time favorites. Nels' tenor voice led in "Throw another log on the fire," and Greg followed deftly, trilling notes the length of the keyboard.

Holly admired his command of music. He was a "pro." Strange, not to know anything more about him, and to be thrown into his company like this. She was relieved that he was occupied, playing for the crowd, and that Chris was with Aunt Midge. When the love songs changed to syncopated rumbles and couples began to jerk and sway around the room, Holly found a lounging divan along the shadowy wall and tried to relax. In the midst of the party she felt utterly detached from the crowd. Closing her eyes she could vision her own crowd of happy skiers back home. They were munching chocolate cake and eating Morrison's famous home-made ice cream. Carol was playing the piano and Janet Eagan was singing about the love of God. Their enjoyment was clean. It was real. They all wanted God in their lives; it was His Spirit of love, joy, and peace which dominated their social times. The two crowds were as different as day from night. *What fellowship* . . . That verse again! Why did it keep popping into her mind?

Ted and Rene changed partners with Nels and Gwen; she heard Ted mention her name and knew he was wondering where she was. In the shadowy edges of the room she slipped around the wall and upstairs.

In the rest room she ran into Aunt Midge. "I let Jessie and Sam use the shower room in the lower level where our private bedrooms are located," she explained to Holly. "Are you having a good time? You look fagged."

"I am," Holly admitted. "Guess I'll wash up before the big rush tonight."

45

Aunt Midge gave her a sharp glance. "They won't retire until early morning. I have to leave tomorrow, but Ted assured me you folks'll get along fine. He is arranging quite a surprise for his guests tomorrow evening. Special music from one of the night spots. Had to pay double to book them for a Saturday night entertainment. Personally, I do not see putting out that kind of money, but the Hollisters have never had to count the cost. Well, you girls have a nice time and don't break any bones on the ski slides."

Holly was relieved to be alone. She took a shower and was debating whether to dress in slacks or pajamas when Liz and Gwen rushed in.

"Holly, darling!" Liz showed consternation. "You aren't going to bed now! Everyone notices your absence and Ted was looking for you. He's crazy about you; you know that. Come down and don't let that brat think she's scored a hit. Everyone has her number."

"I'll say," said Gwen. "And we all marvel that you didn't scratch back."

Holly rejoined the group but the attentions of Ted fell flat. The odor of liquor on his breath nauseated her. She moved about mechanically, doing the things they expected. About two in the morning Liz suggested they all turn in, since a few guests wanted to arise with the sun.

From her bunk in the wall alcove Holly watched the new slice of moon slide in and out of gray clouds. The snowy wooded slopes were a charcoal drawing. She made a mental picture of the scene for future reference. Drifting into sleep, she was conscious of a troubled mind. This ski party was not the thrill she had expected. "Dear Heavenly Father," she began, then hesitated in confusion. What was there to say?

Morning light glared through the glass wall, lifting her eyelids. Her watch said six. The girls were all dead to the world but she heard a stir on the other side of the building. Chris, below her, was an igloo of white wool blankets. Holly drifted into shallow sleep. In another hour the walls reverberated to the sound of a hunter's horn.

"That crazy Ted!" she heard Liz moan. "Waking everyone at this hour!" Moans and sighs along the wall announced each guest. No one stirred from her warm cocoon of covers. At seven-thirty, Chef Sammy struck a gong which echoed throughout the building.

"Haf an hour we serve pancakes, blueberry syrup, sausages, ham, eggs, coffee; c'mon'nd git up!" His cheerful voice lifted the stupor, and sounds of scrambling for the rest room stirred Holly to action. She tumbled over Chris to the corridor carpet and padded in her wool crocheted footies to Liz's room. Each wash bowl was taken. Sheila shuffled in, yawning audibly.

46

"Gonna fly back home, Lizzy," she said. "Find someone to taxi me to the airport."

Liz smiled as she applied her make-up. "No dice, Sheel. No airport this side of Chi. Tired of us?"

Sheila eyed Holly's quilted pajamas. "What an impression *you'll* make!" she snorted. "Looks like a typical small-town Jane." She banged the door and was gone, ignoring Liz' remark. Holly took another look at the girls and wondered at their thin nightwear. At a ski lodge. In the cold wintertime. Gwen wore beautiful satin pajamas but they were too tight. Liz was a Persian princess in an exotic filmy negligee. Holly took down her suitcase to search for her new wool slacks.

"What, Hol?" Liz tapped her on the shoulder. "We don't dress for breakfast. Come, come. You aren't used to bathing beauties. We have a roaring fire down there and the boys should see their girls in something besides bulky knits."

Holly's face turned color. Her quick glances around amused the girls. One called Lou laughed outright. "She looks like a little girl who just hung her Christmas stocking by the chimney. Isn't she rare?"

"Holly's all right," defended Liz. "Just a mite seedy but we're going to re-do her. I have a gorgeous raspberry colored negligee. Do wear it, Hol. You'll look stunning—"

"No, thanks." Holly shook out her wool slacks and chose a white bulky sweater. "I want to get outdoors the minute breakfast is over."

"Are all the McRaes as staunch as you?" Liz laughed but cornered Holly and whispered, "I thought you were interested in a more sophisticated life. And I quote, 'I was an oddball in high school. Preacher's kid—couldn't do anything the others did—wanted to belong.' O.K. Now is your big chance. I wouldn't have invited you to a party of this sort if I hadn't wanted to help you out of your rut. Don't play the goody-goody, Holly. You know that you secretly want to let loose and have a fling—the same as the rest of us."

Do I? Holly pondered after Liz left. She felt the frosty edges of the room. One girl muttered, "Too, too nice," and looked at another girl knowingly, glancing at Holly with a disgusted expression. Holly felt out of place and was unable to make conversation. The others talked among themselves, leaving her out. Again she was isolated. Her brain pounded, *you don't belong here.* Descending the stairs, she saw the fellows in their ski outfits lounging about the fireplace. Most of them had been outside for hours. They weren't in their sleeping wear; why did the girls have to appear so shamefully? Holly couldn't look straight at one of the girls for fear of showing her embarrassment.

Just as breakfast was served Gregory appeared from the wall and

47

Irene Schuster stood at the top of the circular stair. She called, "Hi, there, Teddy bear. Teach me to ski this morning, won't you, darling?"

Holly caught her breath in dismay. How could any girl have the nerve to appear that way? A bathing suit would have covered her more adequately. Shrill whistles proclaimed Rene the sensation of the morning.

"A Greek goddess, no less," declared Ted, lifting her from the floor and whirling her around. She gurgled gleefully and clung to his neck in mock fright.

Sheila purposely stalked before Greg through the cafeteria line, swaying expressively and commenting to the crowd in general. Greg looked past her and smiled into Holly's eyes. He carried his tray to her chair, pulled up a TV table, and arranged things for their comfort.

"Holly, you are an intelligent young woman," he observed. "I am strongly attracted to a girl who is not afraid to be an individual. One maxim Pater instilled is old-fashioned but right: morals are manners. I am almost inclined to pull out of here today. But wait—have you a ski partner? I'm not too accustomed to the sport; could we help each other?"

"I'm scared to death," confessed Holly, her eyes sparkling. "Shall we choose a small slope and practice for awhile?"

"That will be delightful. My dear, I see an avalanche approaching. Let me handle her. Well, well, Sheila. Ready to show your skill on the great white way?"

Sheila held her head imperiously. "You will have to drive me to a train or bus station, Gregory Baines. I don't care how long it takes you away from your *nice* friends here."

"Home to Chicago?" he said between munches. His calmness irritated her.

"Yes—home to Chicago," she repeated, her voice rising. Heads turned and chatter subsided.

"If you insist." Greg turned to Holly. "Isn't this excellent food?"

Holly nodded, aware of Sheila's malevolent look. When Sheila wheeled around to mount the stairs, Gregory looked sorrowful. "This will take all morning," he muttered. "The nearest train is Flatrock. I should ask you to go along for the ride back if it weren't for the unpleasant aspect of the trip down." Their eyes met in mutual amusement and understanding.

10

As Gregory left the lodge, Chris waddled downstairs. Girls ran up to change clothing and no one seemed to mind Sheila's departure. Holly looked through the kitchen porthole to praise the cooks and Chris called, "Hey, Holly, wait up for me. Let's toboggan, O.K.?"

Holly glanced around the empty living room and agreed. She sat with Chris while the girl had breakfast, enjoying her wholesome chatter of sports, school, the Hollisters, and things in general. Chris wore flannel pajamas topped with a flannel robe and tied in the middle like a bulky package with cord. She was easy to look at after the burlesque show.

Somehow, Holly's day looked brighter after her brief chat with Gregory. She poured another glass of orange juice to keep Chris company and all at once a refrain from a favorite song of her mother's flashed through her mind. It sounded so clearly in her brain that she hummed the tune while the words telegraphed, *As you left your room this morning, did you think to pray?* She looked at Chris, startled. "Do thoughts sometimes surprise you? Like a verse from an old song running through your mind?"

"Yeah." Chris poured more syrup. "Sometimes the tune 'Show me the way-ta-go home' drives me batty. It's one of my dad's favorite record albums. Say, Holly. I'd sorta like to try skis. Are you game?"

"I am if you are," Holly laughed good-naturedly. "Is there a private hill for beginners around here?"

"We'll make one. Boy, isn't it peaceful since that sappy Sheila shoved? Whatta character! She's got no class — absotively, posalutely. I heard one of Liz' guests in the rest room say that Sheel is the type of brainless money and you are the type that has real manners although you — "

"Come from an average middle-class village?" Holly smiled at her frustration.

They hurried outside to watch the professionals on the ski run.

49

Holly saw Ted do a graceful slide jump and return to Rene's side. Rene's girations and cries soon ceased to amuse her; she followed Chris to a shallow incline. The crisp air smelled thin and fresh. Pine branches bent under white snow blankets; the birch trees stretched their arms high above, letting the powdery stuff talcum down.

"Isn't this a fairyland? The lodge below us — oh, Chris! See that red bird. Isn't it a gorgeous sight on that sparkling white branch?"

"Yeah." Chris labored on her skis and paused to look, breathing hard. "Wanta go first? My knees chatter."

"Here goes!" Holly slid from the top, skimming smoothly down-grade. The exercise revived her spirit. Chris soon blew out of steam and went indoors. Holly left her skis and took a long hike across the wooded hills. At times she came within view of Ted's friends on the long ski slopes. At one viewing point she could see Ted, apparently massaging Rene's ankle. At the next open space in her rambles she noticed Ted climbing toward the lodge, Rene clinging to him. Now Irene would have an excuse to keep him waiting on her. For the rest of his life.

She stayed outside all morning and reluctantly moved toward the lodge when Sammy's gong called lunch time. Liz and her boy friend announced their intention of teaching her how to ski. Later, she wished that she had declined. The descent was too fast and her heart thumped wildly. She concentrated fiercely on the position of her legs; her feet were spun glass. A white veil swirled around. Miraculously, she landed upright but she lacked confidence. Her knees buckled and she slid to a stop, half sitting in the snow. Liz shouted a salute and flew past. After they returned to congratulate her she felt strong-hearted and adequate for another attempt. On the second try she began to enjoy the sport. Climbing the hill for a third try she saw Gregory. His shoulders sagged but he came to life when he noticed her.

"Holly, are you a picture! Stay right here; don't go away. Don't move. I want a color shot. Man alive!"

"All right," she laughed. "Don't hurry, Greg. I'd like to rest awhile."

After he took several snapshots, Greg mounted his skis. His clumsy attempts amused those who watched. Holly showed him the smaller incline for beginners and they had fun together. The toboggan run kept them busy for the latter part of the afternoon. Finally the blue shadows across the snow darkened. One by one the lodge company drifted back to home base. Liz had put a sign on the wall, "Rest and dress for dinner at eight."

Holly agreed to meet Greg for dinner, then flung herself into her bunk to rest. The lodge slumbered for two hours. She was awakened by sounds of running water and girls' voices from the shower room.

Her watch showed seven-thirty; the sky was cloudy and from the wall of glass the hills looked cold and dark. She shivered nervously. Now for the last evening with Hollisters. They were scheduled to leave for the University campus late Sunday afternoon.

Her coral wool dress which had looked so wonderful in the store, seemed sickly compared to the expensive dresses around her. Liz was sophisticated in her black and silver sheath. Gwen wore white silk crepe with clinging accordian-pleated skirt, an expensive gold neck ornament and arm bracelet her only accessories. All the girls were stunning. *I am the plain Jane. And I thought my new wool dress was so stylish. All it takes is plenty of money. Is that what makes life full to the hilt? Maybe I should snag a rich man. Let's see how Ted is making out with his clinging vine. Is it possible that she'll carry her play acting too far? He said he'd met a lot of girls but —*

Holly arrived in time to join the last in the cafeteria line. Gregory, impressive in evening clothes, stepped over to take her tray. Suddenly she was no longer ill at ease. His calm voice was a great comfort. He spoke with more animation than usual. "Hollister's chef is tops. Isn't this great?"

Holly looked around. "Yes, it is, Greg. Where's Chris? Haven't seen her all afternoon, come to think of it."

"She said to tell you thanks for skiing with her. She and Aunt Midge couldn't stay. What happened to Rene? She seems to limp slightly."

Rene was a sensation in her cherry red dress, sparkling ice jewels at the throat and ears, her frosty hair sailing high around her head. Holly felt weak. She was thankful for the dim lighting along the walls where Gregory seated her. "Talk about color pictures," she said. "Rene makes a *real* one."

"In an artificial way, yes." Greg's manner was relaxed. His eyes drew Holly's attention, for he looked at her with a strange expression. She sensed that he was bewildered. "They're having special talent from a night spot tonight, so I'll be free from the piano. Let's sit and talk. I'm tired, for some reason. Glad Ted has that stereo on something relaxing for once."

"Greg, you play just super. It's a wonder to me that you are in training for the ministry instead of a career in music. How does it all — I mean — "

He smiled. "I'll try to explain. You know, Holly, I hate the piano. Oh, it's relaxing to play along. I don't mind it — but I wouldn't care to make my living at the keyboard. A little of that beat goes a long way with me. I've favored organ — played in our church and all that — which I enjoy. But — I guess it stems from my early years when Pater forced me to practice. A resentment has built within my subconscious mind. Sometimes I become physically ill if asked to play for any period of time. Yet I know he meant well for me — and I appreciate the fact that I *can* play."

"How did you decide to be a pastor? Or am I intruding?"

"Not at all." Greg covered her hand with his huge palm. "Holly, dear girl, you may ask anything — *anything* of me and I shall be happy to be your friend. Will you be mine?" His sincerity touched her. She smiled with her eyes. "I'd be so happy to be friends."

Suddenly she was aware that Ted was coming toward them. As her eyes met his, she felt a thrill of apprehension. Then she felt conspicuous because of her simple dress; her face burned and she was afraid to speak. Trembling, she lifted her coffee cup.

Ted stopped beside her and laid a hand on her shoulder. "Greg, old man, you have a rare and lovely flower here. I've never met another girl quite like Holly McRae. Almost, I am tempted to back out. But, I'm practically at the altar. Rene and I — " his fingers gripped Holly's shoulder as though it hurt him to speak. "We're announcing our engagement tonight." His dark eyes searched hers and she looked down.

Gregory stood and extended his hand. "Congratulations, boy. May I have the honor of announcing this wonderful news?"

"Sure thing. But first — would you be so kind as to relinquish Holly for one moment? I must speak with her in private."

Holly followed Ted behind the stair wall. A ribbon of moonlight streamed through the glass, lighting his face. His attitude reminded her of Jack as he stood there solemnly. She said, "I wish you much happiness, Ted." Her throat ached and the words lacked expression.

He gripped her shoulders. "Darling — believe me — I love you."

"Look, Ted." Her shoulders stiffened against his hands. "In marriage vows you promise to forsake all others. You have a gorgeous blond with brains, wealth, and you're both crazy about each other. What more could you wish?"

His head bent low until she thought he was going to kiss her. "What more?" he echoed softly, "You."

Holly froze. She stared unbelievingly. Then she wrenched free. "I despise you, Ted Hollister," she said vehemently, and ran from him.

11

Holly whirled around the corner to the stairway and paused to recover her senses. Loud music flooded the room. She stood in the shadows, heart pounding fiercely. Contempt made her tremble in every nerve. Then consternation cooled her mind. What had she done? How could she have lost control of herself? What would he think? She was his guest.

Dismay weakened her as Ted approached. He bent toward her. "Please forgive me; I lost my head. You are entirely right — don't feel badly, Holly, *please.*" He offered a handkerchief from a breast pocket. She dabbed at her eyes, handed it back, gave him a smile, and swiftly crossed the space to her chair.

With relief she saw Gregory standing at another table. In a minute her eyes were clear and when he returned she was composed.

A stamping of feet and medley of loud voices below level announced the nightclub entertainers. Ted, passing by, called to Greg, "I'll let you know when — " then admitted a group of musicians who looked handsome in formal tux.

Greg sighed. "Oh, no!" Holly said, "What's the matter? They are certainly fine-looking men."

"Yes, my dear. But I've met this kind of jazz before. By three in the morning we'll be jerking like African witch doctors. There's Chef Sam bringing out the tub of ice. You don't drink, do you?"

"Oh, yes," she said, smiling mischievously. "Ice water, pop, milk, root-beer, and lots of things." She liked the way he smiled. Not in derision, but appreciatively. She knew he was really trying to project himself into her viewpoint. "Actually, Greg, I have no desire for this sort of thing." She waved her hand at the room. "The fun we had outdoors today was the kind of entertainment I like."

"I'm with you all the way. I get a bigger thrill from searching for knowledge, reading a good book, or from semi-classical music played by a top orchestra. And I enjoy nature such as the beauty we saw today. I see you are ready for dessert. They have frozen fruit sherbet. Allow me — but wait. Excuse me, Holly. I see Ted motioning."

Holly watched the chef's wife carry a long tray to the center table. When Ted waved for others to gather around, she moved closer to see an elaborately decorated cake. Their names, Ted and Irene, were raised above pink frosting hearts. Everyone cheered and the boys whistled their approval. Greg made the announcement and the guests were asked to help themselves. Holly avoided the line at the bar, took her piece of cake, and wandered slowly back to her chair. It was obvious that this party had been planned for one purpose.

She felt her cheeks burn while she waited for Greg's return. How ignorant she was of life. The musicians chose a corner and huddled over their instruments, tuning up. When they melted into a relaxed subtle rhythm, couples drifted around the room arm in arm, chatting with friends and forming little groups. The undertow of liquid melody soon caught their feet; couples whirled around in eddies of the rhythmic beat.

Holly sipped the frozen ice with Greg and silently watched the smooth operation clean-up performed by efficient servants. Tables and chairs disappeared; couches were pushed back against the walls; the bright light of the kitchen porthole blacked out and the long room was a dimly lighted dance hall.

Gregory seemed in no mood to participate. He led Holly to a comfortable divan along the dark wall where they sat with heads back and eyes closed. She realized that he had something on his mind; so did she. Before long she dozed. When she looked at her watch dial it gave the hour of midnight. If only she could slip upstairs; Greg's head had dropped to her shoulder and she hesitated to shift the weight.

The atmosphere was charged. In the weird beat of the drums the dancers were bewitched; each one shook and shuddered, twisted and writhed as though in a torment of mind. In the throes of the jungle rhythm she seemed to lose consciousness. In a trance she pictured herself in the car with Ted that day so long ago. Long, long ago. She yielded to the spell.

His kiss aroused her. With a crash of cymbals and eerie shouts from one of the musicians, she came to herself. Greg was gripping her shoulders.

She pulled away. "I've got to go." He reached for her arm but she sped along the wall and upstairs in the dark. She feared his following. There was no place to be alone. "Oh, God, save me. I'm afraid I can't escape this time."

She felt a new power which gave strength to her body. Her trembling subsided. In the shower room she dashed cold water on her face. *I'm not going down. I'll get into my bunk.*

She lay in the slot along the wall, trying to melt into the shadowy part of her bunk; it was useless, for the moon sailed high, sending shafts of light through the plate glass siding. A couple stumbled past; she need not have feared to be noticed, for they were intoxicated. The horror of drunkenness appalled her. Evidently high-class parties were no different from those in slum areas. She heard a cough. Someone was climbing the stair. The drunk couple were not too far gone to realize that someone was coming near. Giggling hysterically, the girl tugged at her partner's arm and led him away.

Holly saw him approach. She closed her eyes and kept quiet. "Holly." Greg's voice was calm and clear.

"Yes?" she answered coolly.

"You won't be able to sleep. Let's take a stroll outside for fresh air. I promise you that my last performance will not be repeated."

"I'll meet you outside in a few minutes." She slipped to Liz's room to dress, then skimmed down the stairway and around the panel to the outside door. She did not smile at Greg. "What kind of an affair do they *call* this?"

"I know what you mean." He looked sober. "It's easy to lose one's head in such an environment. It's a mystery to me. Fine people — excellent company — then a little wine and dance produces inebriates who completely lose all sense of right and wrong. I don't mind a sociable time with friends up to a certain point but this sort of wild party is not for college age level. I am rather surprised at the Hollisters."

Holly thought, *And you are no different at heart.* She said, "Did you ever read the Proverbs?"

"You mean about wine being a mocker? Yes, my dear." He slipped her hand into the crook of his arm. She shivered in the cold night air. "But, Holly, how do you reconcile a book like that as a part of — as you would say — Holy Scriptures? You surely know what a sheik Solomon turned out to be — a harem far beyond that of the richest Arab oil magnate of all time. Connoisseur of the Arabian race horses — world traveler — who could consider *his* words as coming from an authoritative religious source?"

Holly recalled her father's sermons. "Just because he departed from the Lord and ended his days in sin doesn't mean that he wasn't ever close to God. In his youth he asked God for wisdom. And because his prayer was answered, you and I hear about him today in the twentieth century. The name of Solomon is synonymous with the word 'wisdom,' for he was inspired of God when he wrote. You don't accept the fact that the Bible is God's Word, do you?"

"How can I, when there are so many obvious inconsistencies?"

55

"Name one."

"Well, off-hand — anyway, there's the Noah's ark story. Ridiculous. Jonah. Daniel in the lion's den. Stories of miracles which get bigger and bigger."

"I'll bet you have never read the Bible through once, nor read any books which defend the Scriptures, Greg. I remember hearing some famous teachers of the Book — men with several degrees after their names — who accept it as God's Word because they have studied it. One told us about the ark. The dimensions equalled those of our huge battleships. You know how ships today carry tons of cargo — animals, cars, people — *that* is no problem. The miracles aren't, either. I heard a Russian-born professor speak. In his college days he became an atheist. Then he took up the study of astronomy. He said that any honest-thinking man could not see the design in the starry heavens and remain an atheist. It is against all reasoning that the universe has no designer. The tiniest particles — these snowflakes — each little flower — shows evidence of a Creator, a Master Designer. And in my science class this fall the professor admitted, that in the last analysis, there must have been a power "unknown to us" which gave the first life — or the beginning — which brings me to the first statement in the Bible: 'In the beginning *God* . . .'"

She looked up at Gregory. He walked slowly, lost in thought. "I admire your logic, your faith — " he began, then turned her up the hill they had climbed that afternoon. In a windbreak of trees an uprooted oak made a temporary resting place. They sat down and surveyed the lodge below. Intermittent cries from one or more of the musicians reached them; the tempo of the drums seemed to increase in frenzy.

"I do believe in a Supreme Being, Holly. But the idea of Jesus Christ — sent from God to die for the sins — " he faltered as her clear eyes looked up to meet his. "Holly," he defended himself by raising his tone, "it is perfectly normal for young people to want to dance. But — well, Holly, one *can* make mistakes. It isn't actually a sin to dance. If a person goes overboard — it's his own problem. Call it lack of self-control."

"Yes?" She looked beyond him to the sky. The stars sparkled cold and bright and near.

"Confound it, girl, this sort of thing has never bothered me before. I — I'm trying to analyze myself. Seeing all this — " he waved toward the lodge, "through your eyes — gives me an entirely different sort of reaction. I was able to excuse such parties before. But your father — you — it's hard to explain. I mean — I believe you are genuine. You seem to have a spiritual strength which I lack. Your father's prayer came as easy as any normal conversation — as though he spoke to a person in the same room. I have never in my life heard anyone pray like that — like your father did. It has stirred something in my inner senses — like an organ note — a lost chord."

They sat in silence as deep as the surrounding snow. Suddenly he took her hand and said boyishly, a smile twinkling his eyes, "Say, Holly, let's ski in the moonlight. I was just beginning to catch on this afternoon."

12

Feeling like truants, they hurried to the lower level for equipment. "Door's locked," he muttered. "Have to sneak in through the kitchen and down that way." They edged through the main door and glanced at the writhing dancers.

"Looks like the scenes in movies of Indian snake charmers," he breathed into her ear. She was mildly amused at Greg's effort to project himself into her mind's viewpoint. She followed him along the wall to the aisle of the kitchen.

A light turned on ahead of them, revealing Chef Sam's head around a doorway. "What y'all up to?"

"We can't go to bed with that thump-bump, so we'd like to ski awhile. Will it be all right?" Greg beamed on him.

"Well, suh, I'm not sure what Mr. Ted will say, but — go ahead, son. He'p yourself. Take 'em out this door; it's a self-lock. Come back through the main entrance. If it's locked by the time y'all gets back, just ring the bell."

"Just ring the bell," rang through her mind as Holly skimmed over the top of the hill. "Just ring — " she breathed, then stopped breathing. The hill was a glare of ice which crusted the snow; her feet were flying too fast. She skidded; the skis turned sidewise; she scraped a tree and crashed headfirst into the snow. Her right ankle was stabbed with pain. She tried to pull out of the wreck but the pain was excruciating. Her first thought was of school. *How can I go back to school if I can't walk?*

She heard Greg's shout. "Wait!" In minutes he was at her side. "You're hurt." His deep voice was husky. She struggled to get up; he bent down and lifted her. The ease with which he carried her amazed Holly.

"I always thought you looked like a football halfback," she groaned, shaking as from a chill.

"Fullback describes it better, honey. This was my bright idea—

58

should have known better. I've brought you nothing but grief ever since we started from your house." His muttering, reaching her ears through the stabs of pain, steadied her.

No one noticed when Greg carried Holly through the front door to the servants' rooms below level. Jessie found bandages to wrap the limp ankle and Sam agonized over the situation. He opened a bottle of pills and gave one to Holly. "This will ease yo' pain, honey. Now I'd best get holta Mr. Ted. I shore wish his aunt was here."

Gregory looked at Holly with the alarm she felt. Instinctively, they each cried, "Wait." Holly was terrified at the prospect of interrupting their host in the midst of his gala evening. She wanted to get away from Hollister's. Greg voiced her opinion. "Mr. Sam, please don't trouble yourself further. See here. We'd be leaving in a few more hours anyway; I'll take Holly home. We must not endanger her chances of recovery; she must get to a doctor."

"Well, suh — I reckon y'all knows what's best," Sam said.

His wife agreed. "Y'all tells me where to find yo' things, honey, and I'll pack yo' suitcase. We can explain to Ted and Lizabeth in the morning."

Greg wrote notes to Ted and Marsh. When their luggage was ready, he helped Holly into the car and wrapped her in a thick blanket. Jessie waved a farewell and they rolled down the steep hill road to the highway.

"It won't take the car long to get warm, Holly," he told her. "How do you feel now? I'm anxious about your foot; if it is broken it should be set as soon as possible."

Holly dreaded the prospect of going home. She didn't want her folks to know about the turn of events. "Greg —" she began, then hesitated. She felt groggy and fought sleep.

He didn't seem to notice. "Holly, your town is harder to make from here than Chi. Chicago is on the freeway and we can make it in four hours easily. By daylight I can have you in the elevator at our Lake Drive Manor Apartments and Pater will be happy to call our doctor; his offices are in the same building."

"Oh, Greg, I can't do that. Take me to my dorm at State U. I can't possibly impose on —"

"Impose!" he interrupted, turning to look at her. "I am your friend, Holly dear, remember? And I insist on taking care of you. It was my foolish notion to ski in the dark. Amateur that I am, I should have known better than that! The hills were a glare of ice!"

"But that doesn't mean that you must —"

"Now, Holly, you have not been acquainted with the Baines family long enough to realize that we are rational, rugged individualists like yourself. Even if I hadn't been at fault, I would want to take you to Chi with me. Look, dear girl. My stepmother, Lila, never did like Sheila. My father is blind to Sheila's wiles and if I don't get home before — well, it's like this. I was planning to run home today anyway. I don't have classes until Tuesday. You see — we can have you all fixed up and delivered to your dorm by noon Tuesday. And this is a unique way of introducing you to my folks and for them to meet you."

"I really can't think, Greg. I'm quite tired — " Holly heard her voice trail off. *It must be the sedative.* She heard him answer something, then drifted into a deep sleep.

The return to consciousness was a jab of severe pain. "My foot hurts." She groaned, shifting the blankets, and pulling herself around to face Greg.

His hand clasped her gloved fingers. "It will be hard till you get to the doctor. We're almost there, my brave girl. The pain killer has worn off and you'll be needing something more right away. We'll take Lake Shore Drive; I know a shortcut to our apartment. We have a great doctor there and he'll — "

"Oh, Greg," Holly cut in, "I can't do this! My folks can't — oh, I should have — "

His deep voice mastered her. "Holly McRae, this is *my* date and you are with *me*. It is my decision to take care of you, so don't worry. Hear?"

"Yes, only — "

"And don't think about Sheila. I am beginning to realize what awaits me if I continue to condone her factitious behavior. Besides, she is incorrigible. Holly, my stepmother will welcome you with open arms. We have several hours yet before church services. This will be a tremendous surprise. Why, I am more happy and care-free than I can remember — thanks to you."

Holly couldn't think. The words "baffled and bewildered" hammered in her mind. The thump of drums and weird tunes of the night, touring her memory, added to the frustration. She saw the smoky outline of skyscrapers behind the dirty city buildings and streets. Greg's quiet car nosed through the early dawn traffic and soon bore down wider thoroughfares. From the shore drive, Lake Michigan stretched to their right, cold and gray in the morning mist. Her heart beat fast when Greg slowed before an imposing apartment hotel. He turned the corner, drove into a paved alley, and sounded the horn. A door lifted and they entered a spacious garage. She was not prepared for the grandeur of the place nor the service which followed.

A chauffeur took the wheel while Greg rang for a porter. In a short time they had deposited Holly in a wheel chair and rolled her into an elevator. The interior, richly carpeted, gave her indication that Gregory Baines belonged to an extremely wealthy family. She managed to look into her compact mirror and smooth her hair before they reached the fourteenth floor. *What in the world am I doing here?* But it was a relief to be taken care of. She could not bear to tell her own family about her disappointment at the winter retreat.

13

Late that afternoon she awoke from a refreshing sleep. She was reclining among pillows on a lounge by the picture window. The window made a frame for Lake Michigan, a gray-green seascape. The sunshine which awakened her had burst through a heavy cloud bank.

Her leg ached in its stiff white cast. The doctor had been so kind standing there, wrapping miles of sticky white gauze. Greg stood by to help. He too was kind. His stepmother, a short woman, attractive and smart even in her early morning robe, spoke in the softest of soft voices. She had a slight southern accent. Or was it eastern? No matter. Holly wanted to remember bits of conversation which had interested her during those difficult morning hours.

She recalled the great Dr. Baines standing there in his spacious apartment as they entered: tall, white-haired, dignified. His reaction to Gregory's greeting seemed correct but cool. He suggested "the procedure for resolving their difficulty" in the manner of a physician prescribing pills. Then he inclined his head toward her and asked pardon for taking his leave: he must prepare for Sunday morning services and leave for church.

She had made some inane remark about disrupting things on such an important day and Mrs. Baines had laughed with a tinkling sound and assured her, "You are as welcome here today as springtime after the long winter. I was quite bored with life – the same Sunday evening card party" – scheduled, it seemed, at a friend's home, which she would cancel with pleasure as she had not seen "Gregory dahling" for ages. She was relieved to see him with some girl besides "that crude Sheila. I have never once taken a liking to that loud-mouthed creature."

Dr. Baines' brief stay in the apartment at dinner time revealed much to Holly. She could see him as Gregory the First. "We shall use our mental-balance restorer called 'rationalization,' Holly, my child,"

62

he had said loftily after she hobbled in on crutches, supported by Greg. "Your accident brought you here to repose as our guest. There is nothing to be lost in this strange circumstance of life, and everything to be gained. The best education is not found in that little one-horse university of yours, but in broadening your powers and horizons by experience. Tomorrow evening I shall arrange for you to share our box at the opera. Would you enjoy that?"

Holly again felt the thrill of happiness at this prospect. She glanced around the long room, noting the exquisite taste in color and decoration. A small grand piano stood near the picture window on her left. *Why am I again thrown in with wealthy people of fashionable society?* Her thoughts were interjected by twinges of extreme discomfort. The cast was a constant "thorn in the flesh." She twisted from her position to sit up straight and put both legs down. Oh, the misery of such a condition.

Mrs. Baines appeared from behind the jalousies which divided the rooms. Her silvery hair was tinted pale orchid. Was it done specially to blend with the dark purple of her velvet dress? Holly could not but admire the pleasant color combination when the lady seated herself in a gold brocade chair in the shafted sunlight.

Holly smiled and said shyly, "You make a lovely portrait, Mrs. Baines."

The lady smiled in acknowledgment. "My dear, it is good mental therapy to treat one's self to all that modern beauty culture offers. You see — " she smiled, folding her fingers and looking out to the lake, "I unconsciously absorb the atmosphere of the manse. Dr. Baines has influenced me tremendously; he did even before we were married, in the years of his rise to fame when I was his personal secretary — " She paused, glanced quickly at Holly, then resumed her relaxed attitude of looking far away. Her voice was so quiet and refined that Holly felt sleepy.

She roused herself. "Don't you have to prepare for evening service, Mrs. Baines?"

"Oh, dear no, Holly. The doctor feels that Sunday is the best day in the week to hold communion with one's self and with our neighbors. He calls it 'good neighbor night.' We have some gala times, first at one home and then another, or at the club. Cards — bingo — or sometimes we make up a theater party on a Sunday evening.

"Of course we hold to our own social set. The doctor has all sorts of people in his congregation and treats them as equals, except in our social life. He makes appointments to counsel anyone who needs his help. *Anyone,* my dear. If the man or woman or couple needing psychiatric treatment cannot pay the regular fee, he takes it from a special fund provided for this purpose by the more well-to-do members."

Holly was stunned. Her father had never accepted a "fee" for his endless hours of counseling. She said hesitantly, "He counsels — most of the time?"

"Ah, yes. He is recognized by all the leading psychiatrists. Medical doctors often refer their cases to my husband. Dr. Baines is, of course, a doctor of divinity. And, my dear, it is simply divine — the way he helps people help themselves.

"He has studied and read on the subject of self-healing for years; we have both found it a fascinating study, I can assure you. We have seen distressed and disturbed people re-enter society with confidence in themselves. Modern psychological research is amazing, Holly. But enough of this; it must be quite boring to you."

"No, it isn't," Holly said quickly. "My father has studied these subjects and has used his knowledge to good advantage. But he counts on the help of God above all other helps."

Mrs. Baines' eyebrows raised. She coughed in confusion, holding her jeweled fingers before her mouth. Holly thought her voice was a trifle cool when she replied.

"We have fond hopes, you know, of seeing Gregory well-established in this charitable work. It won't take him long to make *his* mark on the world. His father takes much pride in that young man. And, by the way, my dear. Let me tell you that the young lady of Gregory's choice should count herself extremely fortunate. Oh, that rascally Sheila. She doesn't rate in *my* book — and never has since — but that does not interest you. This latest piece of news he tells us — of that grand finale in her comic opera scene at the Hollister's — you may be *sure* she'll stay away from *me*. The doctor may feel it his duty to listen to her grievances but I am washing my hands of the whole affair. Besides — " she bent her head as though offering confidential information — "I know a girl of distinction when I meet one."

Holly felt her face grow red. She smiled back. "I haven't known Greg long. We actually just met. I like him very much as a friend — but — "

"Oh, he'll grow on you. Why, here comes the dear boy. Have a good rest, son?"

Gregory strode across the room to Holly's side. "Yes, thank you, Lila, after a session in the study with Pater." He looked down at Holly. "Well, Miss McRae, I hope you aren't too dreadfully uncomfortable to enjoy the evening. I have some records I'd like to share with you, and perhaps Lila can prevail upon Yvonne to send up some tasty french bon-bons. How about it? Or do you have any suggestions?"

Holly suddenly remembered Janet Eagan. She was right here in Chicago! "Greg, she said, "I'll enjoy anything you like. Do you know

64

that I have a girl friend in the city? Would you folk mind if I called her on the phone?"

"The dear girl!" breathed Mrs. Baines. "Isn't she priceless?"

Greg said, "Why not have her over? Where does she live?"

"That will be perfectly grand," agreed Mrs. Baines. She stood. "Now, will you excuse me, dahlings? I shall phone the caterer."

"Thanks, Lila. Holly, call your friend and then let me talk to her. I'll call a cab and have her here before you know it — unless she lives in the suburbs."

"She's not too far away, I'm sure. The famous North LaSalle Bible Institute. Oh, Greg, you should hear Janet sing. She can play the piano too. Puts in all the runs and harmony you could want. Will you play for her if she comes? And then get her to sing?"

Greg smiled down upon her. "Let me help you to the phone. Then we shall ask her to come."

Just as Holly made connections, she remembered. Janet would discover that she was here and mention it in a letter home. Oh, well, she would have to confess some day; it might as well be now.

Janet agreed to come after the service at North Street Church that evening. Greg offered to meet her in the east lobby while his chauffeur waited with a car. Holly tingled with joy for she was proud to have Janet meet her new friends. She was also aware that talented Janet, with her quiet charm and dark beauty, would appeal to Gregory. *They would make an ideal couple.*

14

While Greg was absent, Holly rested in a big leather lounge chair, her cast stuck straight across the footboard. The maid, Yvonne, arranged the lights for evening and closed heavy draperies to the windows. She offered Holly cigarettes and seemed quietly shocked when Holly refused.

Mrs. Baines tripped in, her spike heels wobbling on the thick rug. She was dressed in a luxurious lavender-gray fur coat and pert hat. "Holly, you younger folk enjoy yourselves tonight. We have a commitment for the earlier part of the evening; I don't expect we shall have to stay late but I have instructed Yvonne to see to your bath and help you prepare for bed. I'm sure you won't wish to stay up as late as you did last night."

"You are quite right, Mrs. Baines," said Holly. She was relieved to be left alone for awhile.

A recording, turned low, soothed her troubled thoughts. Holly rested until Greg and Janet came in. Roused from light sleep, she almost jumped from the chair. The cast clanked and Greg reached a hand to steady her.

"Janet! You look wonderful! School is agreeing with you." Holly admired Janet's shining black hair and was glad she knew how to dress in good taste. The Eagans were like the McRaes, ordinary folk. Since they could not afford expensive clothing, they had to take greater care in the selection of less expensive things. Janet had always looked attractive; tonight she was radiant.

"Oh, Holly, how exciting! A ski jump — a midnight ride with Paul Revere — " Janet stood before Holly and gestured with her hands.

Greg laughed heartily. "One if by land, two if by sea, so they had three lights burning for us in Chicago."

"That's *funny,* Greg." Holly was surprised at his warmth. She had never seen him in such a mood.

The evening was gay from the start. Janet had a song book and

66

played the piano until Greg asked her to sing. Holly was glad to see him open the hymnbook and follow at the keyboard; he could improvise the harmony to "How Great Thou Art" as though he had played it for years. When he didn't know a song she wanted to sing, he asked Janet to accompany herself. She sang several favorites of the young people at LaSalle. "I Am Not Worthy," and another, "It Took a Miracle," brought tears to Holly's eyes. *It touches the lost chord he told me about.*

Holly couldn't help but see that Greg was impressed. He finally was so moved by the music and words of one song that he asked Janet to sing it through once more. When she finished he said, "These aren't merely religious songs; they seem to make Jesus Christ a real Person — as though you knew Him today — not as a person from the pages of history."

Janet turned from the bench and looked at him. "He *is* real. He lives today because He not only died for my sins — and yours — and for the whole ungodly world — He arose from the dead, the Mighty Conqueror." Then she smiled. "There goes another song. We'll save that for another time. What I want to say is this: God is real. His Holy Spirit speaks to my spirit that I belong to Him. He is a reality in my life because I have come to Him through the Person of His Son, the Lamb of God who atoned for my sins with His own precious blood."

Gregory looked amazed. He walked around, hands behind his back, then stopped and stared at her. "You speak of sin. Surely, *you* girls do not need to worry your pretty heads over such a sordid subject. A girl like you — and Holly — *I don't get it.*"

"Here is the way it works." Janet spoke with confidence. "You and I have to agree with God that we aren't much. That is, we are not fit to enter His presence even when we are doing our best. We have to admit and confess that we don't measure up to *His* standard of holiness. Is that right?"

"Yes, yes of course. But — " Greg shrugged his shoulders and looked at Holly with a puzzled expression, then back to Janet.

"All right." Janet crossed the room, picked up her Bible, and turned to the Book of Romans. "Read it for yourself, here in the third chapter. 'All have sinned.' Do you agree with God this far?"

"No, I do not." Greg walked away from the Book. "Some — yes, perhaps many, do things they shouldn't. They go to excess. Sin is a lethal word. It is for the poor devils in the gutter who haven't had what it takes to make good and useful lives. I agree with the old-time scholars on the premise of the golden mean. Moderation in all things — self-control — a manly fight for self-respect and the esteem of others."

"And do you always have the strength, in yourself, to win the fight against what you know is wrong?" Janet asked courteously but sincerely.

Gregory stopped short. A strange look passed over his face. Then he waved his arm toward Holly and said jauntily, "No, I don't. But she does. She has what you are talking about. Another spirit. What I can't understand is — what gives you two such assurance? *You* aren't from a preacher's family like Holly, are you?"

"No," laughed Janet. "But I'm a Christian."

"A — what?"

"A Christian. I received Christ as my Saviour and now I am a follower of Christ."

"Oh." Greg thought for a moment. "In that category I might not qualify. Strange. Now that is a thought-provoker. We think of America as a Christian nation. But how many of us are following the teachings of the greatest Man who ever lived?"

"Now you're catching on," Holly encouraged him.

The time passed too quickly. Greg left to take Janet back to school, and Yvonne came to assist Holly. Even in her discomfort and fatigue, Holly felt a sense of gladness which she had not known for a long time.

When the time came to leave Tuesday morning, Holly accepted Mrs. Baines' invitation to return for a weekend.

"But I'll wait until this cast is torn off," she said.

"We'll be looking for you," Dr. Baines announced in formal, professional tone. "Good-by, Greg. And I shall expect you to think carefully of the matter we discussed."

The white car glided down Lake Shore Drive. Greg was silent and Holly lost in thought. *For a minister's family the Baines' were a strange couple. Not a word of thanks to God at meals. Not one Bible in evidence. Yet they had confidence that they were doing a good work.* "Many will say to me in that day, Lord, Lord, have we not . . . in thy name done many wonderful works? And then will I profess unto them, I never knew you: depart from me, ye that work iniquity." Words from the Book of Matthew came to mind. *It's natural,* Holly thought vaguely, *that verses from the Bible float through my memory; I've memorized Scriptures from childhood. This is the reason why Greg repeats the things that he knows. But surely he sees the vast difference in our two families.*

A letter from Janet Eagan was on her desk in the dorm when Holly returned. "Dearest Holly. How you do it, I'll never guess. Getting acquainted with such *big* people and making such an impact for Christ. Greg talked about you and what a wonderful family you have, all the way to his home and back to LaSalle. He is a prince of a person. Don't you feel like a princess — riding in a gilded coach? Wait till I tell Carol and the others. Chauffeurs. Hors D'oeuvers. French maids. The works—" Holly laughed aloud.

Liz and Gwen were delighted to see her and helped by contacting her professors and bringing her books and homework. They helped her to the dining hall at mealtime. The days were full, the nights hard to bear although Gwen took the top bunk. Letters from home were full of local news. Her folks were making big preparations for her home-coming at Christmas.

She saw little of Greg for he was in midterm exams in the seminary. *He might be a prince charming to Janet but he certainly isn't to me.* Majoring in psychology! A carbon copy of Dr. Bruce Baines the Great. She hoped Greg liked Janet well enough to see her again.

15

Just before the Christmas holidays, Holly was delivered from the cast. The same evening a call came for her. When she answered the hall phone she heard Greg's deep voice.

"Lila keeps asking me when you are coming to visit again, as you promised. She would like to see how you walk around like other people. So — how about another drive to the windy city with me? This time it will be more comfortable for you." When he noticed Holly's hesitation he said, "Please, Holly. It's been utterly lonely. And just to make sure you'll come, I'll tell you what I'll do. Sunday morning I'll go to Janet's church with you. She asked me to be sure to visit sometime and I thought it looked extremely interesting when I walked in there that Sunday night. O.K.?"

"I'm afraid I can't refuse, Greg. I have no excuses to offer. But — I'll tell you what. I'll go to church with your folks and you go to North Street with Jan. Don't you think that would please your family a lot?"

"Well — yes — but I know they wouldn't mind if you went with me. We'll discuss it on the way. Holly, I'm so glad you're coming. I'll be over there Friday around four and we can eat somewhere on the road."

Holly looked at the phone after she hung up. *Maybe I shouldn't go. But no, Greg is really lonely. Since Sheila. And he will visit the North Street Church this way. I'll call Janet and make sure she understands and meets him there. They would make quite a pair.*

Holly was in high spirits on the trip. As they sat at dinner in a roadside restaurant she began to notice Greg. He was quieter than usual. And he didn't talk to her in his former pompous manner. He seemed different, somehow. She found herself enjoying his company for the first time.

The Baines'. apartment came into focus as Holly revisited. Free from pain, she noticed more. French designed furnishings, gorgeous antiques, massive crystal chandeliers, and deep, deep carpeting.

Mrs. Baines gave her a cordial welcome but Holly felt a definite hostility in the doctor. His greeting chilled her. Mrs. Baines seemed to notice for she immediately went into a rapturous conversation on their plans for Gregory's graduation.

Later in the evening after his folks retired to their rooms, Greg played records for her. She was glad he liked harmonies from *Oklahoma* and the *Grand Canyon Suite.*

"Holly," he said, with brown eyes twinkling, "let's not wait until Sunday to see Janet. I have a friend in the city; let's double for dinner tomorrow night. We could go sight-seeing first, in the afternoon, and take Janet with us."

"If you are Janet's date, all right."

"What do you mean?" Greg clasped her hands in his massive palms. "You'd rather not be mine?"

Holly was surprised. "That's not what I meant. Janet isn't the kind of girl who will go on a blind date. No matter who he is. She may not consider dating you either. She's — well — a spiritually minded *individual.*" She smiled as she thought of the right word to show Greg what she meant.

"I see. Well, there is one way to find out. You call her, Holly, and then let me explain it to her."

It turned out as Holly predicted. They had a difficult time persuading Janet to double date. Greg finally hung up and turned to Holly.

"'I'll be happy to sight-see in the afternoon,' she says. 'But I'm in exams here and really should be back by six at the latest.' She was tactful. A very nice girl. Blamed it on exams."

Holly laughed. "If she said she had exams, then she *had* 'em. Jan tells the truth."

"We'll go to dinner anyway. Just the two of us. Why didn't I think of it before? You have never dined at the Regent. I'll make reservations for the Victorian Room. You'll love it." He picked up the receiver, looked over his shoulder at her, and set it down. He came to her and bent his head. "May I take you to dinner, Holly?"

His humble attitude shook her. It was unlike him. "You know I'd love to, Greg. But I'm disappointed about Janet. And it would have been nice for you to see this friend."

"The only friend I am thinking of right now is a lovely girl by the name of Holly McRae."

Sitting at a cozy table for two, Holly marveled at the regal atmosphere. The Victorian Room was a dream, dimly lighted by high chandeliers. Her feet had seemed to sink inches in the carpet as she walked to their table. White-coated waiters glided soundlessly among the tables, trays balanced on one hand. An ensemble played softly from a round platform along the center wall. She recognized *Holiday for Strings.*

"This is beautiful," she said softly, glancing around at the rich furnishings.

"This?" He smiled; his brown eyes held hers for a long moment until she dropped hers in confusion. She read something deeper than loneliness and caught her breath. Was he expecting something more from her than the friendship? *This will be my last trip to his home. I can't encourage Greg!*

It was during their entree that she saw Jack Martin. Just as she saw him, he turned his head and their eyes met. Jack dropped his napkin, said something to the girl with him, and came toward her. Holly was shocked. He looked as though he belonged in this sort of world. He was more handsome than ever but he looked older. His expression showed him a man-of-the-world; gone was the wounded boy.

"Holly McRae! Is it you — here in Chicago — or am I dreaming again?" He bent over to look straight at her.

"Yes, it is, Jack. I want you to know my friend, Gregory Baines. Jack Martin is a good friend of mine from home."

Gregory stood, shook hands, and Holly felt the electric connection.

Jack said, "Won't you two join us? We are two couples and we're heading for the 'Shore' after dinner. It's an exclusive club but I could get you in."

Greg said drily, "I have a membership in all the clubs here. Live on the Lake Shore."

Jack nodded and looked sharply at Holly. "That's fine then. Please join us, won't you? Holly and I skipped rope together as kids. Yes, waiter. Would you mind changing this couple to my table? It's the one by the wall."

Holly was amused to see Jack's salesmanship in action. He had them on the dotted line before they had actually said yes. She sensed Greg's disappointment but she was grateful for the turn of events. It would keep their conversation from getting too personal. And it was good to see Jack the way she remembered him in high school.

When they were seated at the larger table, Holly followed Jack's introductions. "This is Cheryl, one of our employees at Patterson Plate Glass." A thin, black-eyed girl with bleached white hair like Rene Schuster's.

"Randy and his wife, Babs, also from Patterson." Randy, a distinguished appearing man, graying at the temples, whose pretty wife reminded Holly of Mrs. Baines. Only Babs was much younger. Holly was glad they were the refined type.

Later that evening she wondered. At the night club they all drank or smoked constantly, told the typical shaded stories, and behaved much like the revelers at Ted's lodge. Holly became uneasy to the point of discomfort. *I don't belong in this crowd. I must leave at once.*

Greg seemed to understand. He announced, "Let's go, Holly. It's church tomorrow. Remember?"

Jack swept Holly aside and made her give him her address at State University. "You are the only girl I've ever cared about. You've *got* to write to me. I'm making money, Holly. I'm going places. In this business the sky's the limit. This girl is Bab's favorite at the office and she made the date for Cheryl to go with us — said that I was working too hard and she never sees me with a girl — and she wanted to make two couples for an evening out. See?

"Honey, I'll be home next week for Christmas and we'll have a long talk together. What say?"

His eyes compelled her to answer. Holly felt the impact of his dynamic personality and almost yielded to the enchantment of the moment. Suddenly his smoke-laden breath suffocated her.

She smiled and turned away. "Be seein' you," she said lightly, and was relieved to take Greg's proffered arm.

"I don't expect you to understand this," she told Greg on their way out. "But I'm through looking for something in life I thought I'd missed: it's people like these who are missing the biggest thing in life — life in the third dimension — because they have no capacity for enjoying life beyond the things of the body and soul. There's no spirit. No consciousness of God. So there's no spiritual life. And no desire for anything better than their filthy little jokes. You know where the conversation runs — you know what I mean, surely."

"I'm with you there, Holly, dear friend." Greg sounded sincere. "And I am understanding your viewpoint a little bit better as time goes by."

16

Mrs. Baines was so thrilled at the idea of Holly's visiting their church that she agreed with their plan for Greg to meet Janet Eagan at LaSalle Institute. "And bring her back with you, Gregory, if she is free to come," she said graciously.

Greg did not bring her back. He explained to Holly. "I met her as she came down from the choir after church. She had a date to sing at a Senior Citizens' home at three o'clock, so she couldn't come this far out of her way. I asked her why she couldn't let someone else take her place when her girl friend was here only for the weekend. Do you know what she said?"

"I can guess." Holly smiled at him.

"She said, 'In all my decisions, it's a matter of putting Christ first, above me and my desires.' She said that God is not a myth to her. She said she worships this God and is so full of His Spirit of love for others that she can't miss one opportunity of telling others about Him. So I notice, Holly, now that I'm here, she was telling me all this about God for my benefit, perhaps. What a diplomat!

"And did I have a double-barrel leveled at me this morning! I heard more about God and the Bible at this North Street Church than I've heard all my life. How did you like the Pater?"

Holly shivered. The clammy atmosphere of the great cathedral she had attended left her dead in spirit. The choir chanted anthems as lifeless as dirges. She had listened to Dr. Baines discuss brotherhood, the coming world church of which he heartily approved, and his favorite subject, psychiatry, all rolled into one oration. It hadn't lasted long; she and Mrs. Baines were home an hour before Greg arrived. The doctor had to see someone about his broadcasts.

She looked at Greg, deciding not to mention that she had been bored. "He is well-informed on his subject," she said. "Of course I am not used to hearing the type of messages he gives in a church

74

service. It seems more like sitting under one of my professors at school."

Gregory looked across the big lake. Furry snowflakes stuck to the picture window. "Yes, I know," he said briefly.

Mrs. Baines had ordered a fine dinner and had the table set in formal style. Yvonne was absent; another maid served. Holly enjoyed the dinner but was depressed. She tried to shake the feeling by entering their conversation at every opportunity.

Finally it was over. Dr. Baines coughed slightly, leaned back and announced: "I am taking Miss McRae on a little tour through my church, Gregory. I wish to show her my study and the broadcasting studio. We shall be back in approximately an hour."

Mrs. Baines looked her surprise. Greg was stunned, Holly knew. Why was his father leaving him out of this? It was strange. She followed the doctor to the car. He was polite but distant; she felt his stern, uncompromising attitude. He said little until they arrived at the cathedral where he kept his word by showing her through the building; then he asked her to be seated in the outer office to his study.

He stood by the long mahogany desk, lit a cigar, and puffed in silence. Presently he walked to the window and back, looking down at the carpet. She was relieved when he said something to her.

"Miss McRae." *Puff puff puff.* He took more long, careful strides back and forth. She had a queer sensation of being a witness in a courtroom. He acted like a lawyer.

Finally he began. "It will be useless for me to delve into an explanation of apperception; you could scarcely be expected to follow me." *Puff puff.* "Let me put it in the words of a great poem you have no doubt read. *Ulysses.* 'I am a part of all that I have met.'" He paused, puffed, resumed his strides.

Holly quoted, "'Yet all experience is an arch where-thro' gleams that untravell'd world, whose margin fades forever and forever when I move.'"

"Yes, yes, quite right. I see you know your literature. Now where was I? Ah! We are a part of all that we have met. You are what you are and who you are, Miss McRae, because of past associations and environment. My son, Gregory, will graduate this coming June and is already bound to a new experience — a coveted position in this city — which I have managed for him — of the sort in which I am now a leader.

"My son, as you may know, was engaged to a highly capable young woman, Miss Sheila Strand. Her personality complements that of my son's; he has always been more or less docile, unfortunately, like his mother — who is dead." *Puff puff puff.* "Miss Strand

75

is not always understood by the common layman because of her explosive will. If you had studied into these matters of the mind, my dear, you would not have been prejudiced against her, nor have influenced my son to be prejudiced. He has unconsciously turned to you since Sheila went into one of her temperamental stages and — uh — "

Tantrums, you mean, Mr. Holly took in the meaning of the lecture and felt her face grow hot.

"Sheila's is the normal type of character," he went on. "All humans would be more stable, emotionally, if they would cast off all inhibitions — the fears that obstruct a person from being himself. Miss McRae, Sheila has spent years preparing for the role she will assume with my son at her side. She has studied advanced psychology under my supervision and has the background — a 'total adjustment,' as we say; therefore she understands the type of work in which they will soon be engaged.

"Her impulses are prompt but she has the courage to accept their consequences and the intellect to succeed in spite of them. She is far better equipped to counsel others than the inhibited girl with scruples, fear of consequences, or narrow mental outlook."

Holly stood to her feet, her eyes sparking. "Sir, I understand very well what you are trying to say. I don't want to hear any more. If you call this 'work' the ministry, why do you carry it on in a church building? You are not counseling people in God's Word and your reasoning is contrary to His; God doesn't look at it that way."

She saw his eyes narrow and braced herself for his retort. He removed the cigar from his mouth and was about to speak when they heard a tap on the door. It opened and Sheila sauntered in, her crimson mouth curved in a disdainful smirk.

"My future daughter wished to say a few words to you, Miss McRae. We shall not keep you much longer." Before Holly could think to answer, Dr. Baines opened a door behind the desk and closed it after him. She was alone with the leering girl.

"What I have to say should interest you, Holly McRae," she said, affecting Dr. Baines' professional tone. "It should also help to turn your affection to a more hopeful subject. No, no, don't interrupt. I arranged for this interview with you and I intend to have it. My dear, Gregory belongs to me by right of a wife. The removal of an engagement ring does not alter the fact that he and I have been quite close; he knows as well as I that he can't throw me over. I'll tell any girl he ever dates that he — "

"That's enough!" Holly turned to the outer door, then hurried back to the chair where she had dropped her purse.

"You'll find the door locked." The dry-ice tone brought Holly to

76

a shocked standstill. Before she could recover, Sheila went on. "No one could fit into this picture — " she waved a hand, indicating the doctor's domain — "as well as I."

Holly broke in. "Greg should be the one to decide that."

Sheila's suave voice altered. In a shrill tone she snapped: "You think that because you're a self-righteous little prude you'd make a minister's wife. Let me tell you something." Her voice lowered. "Dr. Baines' first wife, Greg's mother, was a religious fanatic like you who called herself a 'Christian believer.' She talked constantly about Jesus Christ and His sacrifice on the cross. Even thought He had been raised from the dead. She was so wrapped in these delusions of the mind that she'd start praying out loud in the middle of the night for God to save her husband from the 'error of his ways.'"

"How do *you* know she did?" Holly said mildly, putting on her gloves.

"Because about that time I started classes under Dr. Baines at his temple. He began to open my eyes to the modern rational way of thinking. And his secretary, Lila, the present Mrs. Baines, arranged for me to meet her boss's son. I know them all intimately. She was as concerned about the doctor's wife as he was."

"This has nothing whatsoever to do with me, Sheila. So if you will come to the point — "

"It has everything to do with you!" Sheila's face flamed red and her voice shrilled higher. "Can't you see how successful Dr. Baines is today — with a modern wife who doesn't make him ashamed of her in public? Anyone who is dumb enough to hark back to the Bible as an authority ought to be put in an institution for the insane, the same as they did his first wife when they — "

The inner door flew open and Holly saw Dr. Baines stand there; his face was a mask of wrath.

17

"You recorded loud and clear on the intercom, Miss Strand," he hissed through set teeth. He advanced slowly, deliberately, holding Sheila still by will power. "You haven't the sense of a moron. Where did you get such an idea? You are the one who should be committed to an instit—"

"Just try it and see!" Sheila blazed back. "Years ago Lila gave me two wastebaskets to take to the incinerator and I found some *very interesting* correspondence between you and Lila. I've got it yet!"

A ring of white circled his mouth. Holly held her breath in fear. His menacing attitude made Sheila back to the wall.

"You moron!" he breathed heavily, as though he climbed steep stairs.

Holly edged toward the door to his study. She must escape. He was insane with fury. She felt instinctively that he would turn on her after he dealt with Sheila. A quick backward look at the girl gave her the feeling of watching a cobra swaying before a deadly enemy, ready to strike. Then she slipped into the doctor's study. She looked from one wall to another for a door. There. Across the room. She ran to open it but stopped short. It was only a closet for wraps. She was trapped. Moving back to the outer office door, she stood shakily, listening, afraid her loud heartbeat would remind them of her presence.

Sheila's ironic retort reached her clearly. "What brought this outburst? To quote your own lecture, 'The man who is possessed by anger is not *self*-possessed.'"

He towered over Sheila, his head lowered like an angry bull. He visibly swayed as the cobra struck.

Holly suddenly recalled his words to her of moments ago: "Her impulses are prompt but she has the courage to accept their consequences . . . she is not always understood because of her explosive will." Holly smiled nervously. Dr. Baines was receiving a dose of his own prescription.

Sheila's logic dashed cold water on the pressure built up in his mind; the doctor's pride in his own philosophies spouted steam as the pressure suddenly sagged. But Holly felt his wrath taking another form as he spoke.

His voice was still thick but not so guttural. Did she discern a thin oily tone as he said, "You are evading the issue — Sheila — cleverly evading. Miss McRae!" Suddenly he whirled to face Holly, keeping a massive hand on Sheila's shoulder. "You are my witness. That's all I need. A witness. You heard this woman say with her own tongue, 'I stole correspondence of yours.' She stole personal correspondence. *Didn't* you hear that?" His eyes gleamed desperately.

Sheila suddenly wrenched from his grasp and slapped him a stunning blow in the face. His glasses flew. He lunged and reached for her, his hands outstretched but Sheila, like a serpent, writhed from his grasp and ran in circles until the doctor followed her behind the massive desk.

Quicker than he, she snatched her keys and unlocked the hall door before he could catch her. His mouth was no longer white; his face flamed dark red. He struck out but she raced down the hall.

He shouted in gasps, "I'll get my lawyer. I'll see to you."

Holly wanted to run out, but the big man blocked the door. Then he staggered, pressed one shaking hand to his head and another to a limp shirt front. Was it a heart attack? Blindly he reached for something to hold to and, without realizing it, Holly stood by to help steer him to a chair.

She bent to recover the glasses. He polished them absent-mindedly, neither of them commenting on the cracked lens or his shaky hands.

He mumbled, "Better call Greg to — no, no. Better not. I'll drive you back." Still puffing, he flung on his overcoat and reached for his hat. Holly followed him mechanically as he stalked out to the car. She listened to his denunciations of Sheila. "She's a raving maniac," he repeated several times.

With great relief Holly arrived at the apartment hotel and found Greg packed and ready to leave the city. Lila's eyebrows arched high when the doctor slammed the door from the hall. Holly, following him, saw Greg's look of surprise.

Dr. Baines threw his hat on the console table and swore. "Gregory, I insist that you have nothing to do with that wily snake-in-the-grass, Sheila Strand. She's had me fooled. Lila, you were right; she's a low-class boor. Liar! Swindler! I'm cutting off all business with Strand's. I'll fix her!"

Greg stared in astonishment and started to speak but his father lifted one of his cases and strode to the door. "I'll see you off, son. Miss McRae, my apologies for the nerve strain you have undergone.

You can see for yourself that a little minx like that — that — "

"Father!" Greg's voice cut in. They entered the self-service elevator. Since others were in the car Dr. Baines tried to whisper but his anger prevented his voice from lowering. Holly heard the words "frame-up" and "have nothing more to do with her, do you hear?"

Then they were in the basement garage where people were coming and going. The doctor pumped her hand, looked hard at his son, and they were off.

They had not gone a block before Greg cried, "What happened! For the last two visits Pater has been admonishing me to make up with Sheila and now he's blown his fuse over something. I've never seen him angry because of her although he should have been many times. But you — Holly — were as white as a ghost when you came in. I've got to know!"

Holly repeated all that she had witnessed. When she told him of the conversation between Sheila and herself, and of the words which brought his father rushing into the outer office, Greg began to shake. His body shook; his arms trembled. Finally he was forced to stop the car by the curb. Holly was fearful when he laid his head upon his arms over the wheel and did not speak but kept shaking.

She said, "It didn't surprise me — what Sheila said about you and her — I've recognized for some time that you have the same philosophy of life as Ted and Liz and many others in the university. I'm beginning to see that such a life is not for me. But Sheila was wrong if she thought I was after you. Such a thing has never entered my mind — least of all *now*."

She was alarmed at his shaking; his back heaved as he groaned. She put a gloved hand on his arm. "Greg, don't. There's no need — it's all right — ."

"It's — not — all right." The words seemed wrenched from his soul "It — never — has been."

She waited for him to recover. When he lifted his head she felt sick at heart for him. His face was wet; his eyes looked straight ahead.

"It is all true. If you despise me it is no more than I despise myself. Holly — "

She waited for him. When he spoke, his voice was low but steady. "I've known this story about my own mother — heard it from P — from *him* since I was about thirteen years old. But I've never seen it — in this light — before. He really sold me on the idea that she was mentally off balance." Again his voice broke. They remained silent for a time. Then, "Since I've met your family I have seen what real Christians are. They are more 'balanced' than the rest of us." His tone grew bitter. He started the motor; they rolled along the freeway leading from the city.

"What a fool I've been." Greg spoke as though to himself. After another long silence she heard him give a gasp like a half-sob and he spoke in an anguished tone: "How she must have suffered. Only God knows how much — and for how long."

Holly saw his cheeks grow wet and began to realize that she was witnessing another tragedy in life. After a long time she said softly, "I understand, Greg. You have never realized — until now — just how it was."

"I believe in God." His hard, bitter tone gave her the feeling that he had not heard what she said. "I believe in the kind of God your father believes in. He must have been *her* God, too." After awhile he went on: "At least, your folks' philosophy of life gives them a heart. A different spirit. As you and Janet have shown me."

Hours passed as they sped down the highway, each lost in thought. Holly began to grasp the full import of the story. Greg's mother — the victim of a sinister plot!

"Greg," she said huskily, "do you know what it means to be a Christian? It's just as you said. You have a different spirit. When I told God that I loved Him because He first loved me and sent His Son to take the punishment for my sins — this happened when I was just a child — you know, immediately I was conscious of His Holy Spirit. I can't explain it, but it's real. Anyone who believes that Christ died for his sins and that He rose again from the dead, and asks God to save him from his sins — the Bible declares that God's Spirit dwells in that person and makes him new inside out. It isn't a religious cant or creed — as you seemed to think. It is a person: Christ in my heart and life.

"And you know, Greg, I was afraid to show that I was different — when I first came to State U. So I hid — I hid my light — didn't talk to God or read my Bible or pray. I wanted to see if I had been missing something all these years. But Greg — it is these ungodly people who are missing life. It's just as the Bible says. Those who live in sin are dead while they live. Dead to God and alive only to themselves."

Greg nodded. "That's what happened to my parents. My mother knew God and my father has always thought only of himself. He has preached the 'self-healing powers of the mind' all the days of my life. Yet he has been mighty hard to live with. I've looked up to him in a — well, a sort of awe — I guess. I've never once felt a deep bond between us. With him, love is an emotion — a word, merely. And 'rational thinking' does away with our emotions. I see. I see. Holly, my father withheld love and compassion from my mother. It was a battle between him, his selfish philosophy, and my mother who believed in God. His lack of love is what killed her. *He killed her.*"

Holly winced. She tried to think of something to say which might help him escape the gall of bitterness. She feared the hardness in his voice and the steely look in his eyes; he stared straight ahead.

After a long time she said, "The first Bible verse I memorized when I was hardly two years old was this one: 'God is love.' You know, Greg, I am just now realizing what this means. *His love keeps our hearts in the right attitudes.* I can remember many times when I ran away from Him and hated to hear the Bible read at our table. And every time I ran away, nothing went right. I was perfectly miserable. I tried to have a good time with the worldly crowd in high school, but for some reason I couldn't enjoy it. When I'd get alone — away from the gang at school — I felt God's love in my heart pleading for me to respond.

"And Greg, I am telling you the truth: when I turned a deaf ear to Him I was unhappy even while I played along with the crowd. But each time I responded to His Spirit, I had such relief from my *self*. I actually had joy down in my heart. This is proof, isn't it, that God does make a person new by putting His own Spirit within. He gives you a new dimension so that you stand out from the world and view it as He does. You wish that everyone would recognize Him and how great He is. Oh, Greg, I am so ashamed that I haven't stayed close to Him always. It could have happened to me — if I had met a man who didn't have God's Holy Spirit in his heart — and I had married — "

She stopped in confusion when he turned quickly to look at her.

"You — your family — and Janet — are the only Christians I have ever met. Will you pray for me, Holly?"

"Now?"

"Yes."

Holly bowed her head. With closed eyes she spoke. "Dear Father, I'm sorry for the way I've felt about Thee and the way I've distrusted and dishonored Thee. I want to thank Thee for always forgiving me — for Jesus' sake — and because He paid the debt of sin I owe. And, dear God, help Greg. Help him to turn from all this — that hurts — to the only One who can give comfort and peace to his soul. In Jesus' dear Name, Amen."

"Thank you," he said softly. His eyes were misty; his expression had softened.

"You know?" she said, a smile in her voice. "I feel so greatly relieved somehow. I can't explain it — it's like I said before. His Spirit is able to commune with mine; it's like a reunion. Now that I've confessed everything to Him that He knew already, we can begin to enjoy life together again."

"Do you know some of those songs Janet was singing, Holly? The one about how great God is?"

"'How Great Thou Art'?" she asked.

"Yes, that's it. Sing it. Can you?"

"Some of it. But I can't sing, Greg. Not like Jan."

18

After the fast moving events of that Chicago weekend, Holly found studying impossible. Fortunately there were no exams the week before Christmas.

Her father wrote, mentioning a letter he received from Gregory. She couldn't help comparing her father's attitude with that of the Chicago pastor's when she read: "My dear daughter, Holly, Christmas is here at last, bringing you home for a high mark on our calendar — your birthday and our celebration of the first coming of Him who loved us — our Lord Jesus Christ.

"Holly, I can't begin to tell you how we've held you up in prayer, night and day. That day you left for the weekend up north, even Timmy broke down and cried. He was afraid his sister would come back to us a different girl. Mother expressed more faith in God than the rest of us; she said we had brought you up to know the Lord as your own Saviour and Friend, and she was counting on God to keep you.

"But I was fearful of your falling into some situation which would be hard to overcome. You see, honey, it's as the Book says; the same temptations come to all of us. I know what they are — I've run the gauntlet of temptation for all these 'pleasures of sin' which, God says, last only for awhile. I thank God that He gave me the victory; but we have to realize that a person must *will* to go God's way. I had to make up my mind to turn from these sins of the flesh to follow Christ. Yes, His Spirit in us gives us the desire to do God's will; and the power is there to go God's way in any given situation. But a Christian can fall into sin if he or she stubbornly goes on in a course of self-will as in the case of Kings Saul or David. I prayed far into that night, Holly. You are an adult but we love you in the same way that we did when you were younger — and always will.

"Thank you for writing us so faithfully each week. We've prayed often for the young people you mentioned, especially Gregory. He has potential. I can't disclose the contents of a personal letter he has written but can say that he wants an appointment with me. We look for him to drive down shortly after Christmas."

Holly could guess the reasons for Greg's need of counsel and she knew *this* pastor would be able to help him. *I am a part of all that I have met . . .* She whispered a prayer: "Father in heaven, Greg met my folks and now we pray that as a result of this he will meet Thee as his Saviour. Help Dad to know just what to say to him when Greg comes over from Chicago. In Jesus' dear Name, Amen."

Next day Holly heard from Jack Martin. Liz, who had definitely cooled toward her in the few weeks since Thanksgiving, thawed considerably when she saw the blood-red roses.

"Who do *you* know in Chicago, chick?" she cried eagerly.

"Oh, a guy," Holly smiled sweetly, holding one of the roses to her face. She felt her cheeks turning a brighter color.

"Well, kitten, I suppose you know what he means by this red-red-red?"

"Oh, yes," Holly said lightly. "I've known for some time that he wants to marry me."

Liz yelped and Gwen appeared from across the hall with other girl friends. Holly once again felt the warmth of their friendliness and glowed from their attention. Mischievously, she held an envelope high over her head and told them, "I'll introduce you to him next Wednesday if you're here when he arrives. He's driving me home for the holidays."

"When will he get here?" they asked.

"About noon."

Some of the girls whooped and others groaned in mock disappointment since they had to leave earlier.

For everyone in the dorm, time crawled. The rooms were a wreck from strewn suitcases and clothing. The dorm mothers ceased their scoldings about loud voices, for the holiday mood caught them all. Wreaths and bells danced in the windows and the old familiar melodies lifted their spirits from the mundane drone of study.

Finally the day of liberation dawned. It was a debonair Jack Martin who appeared on campus. Holly was relieved that he came early. She caught the admiration in the eyes of the girls as she introduced him around. Everyone was sorting luggage and packing cars outside the dorm. Then she noticed the red car.

White-walled tires spun in the circular drive and Ted Hollister leaped out. Liz called from the door. Her cases in hand, she stumbled into the bevy of girls.

Jack Martin graciously stepped forward to assist her and Liz stared at him. He was downright handsome. He was taller than her brother,

Ted, and quite evidently a man who knew his way around. His voice was well-modulated.

"May I help you? Now which way? This car? Oh. don't mention it. My pleasure. Are you one of Holly's friends? Yes, I'm Jack Martin. So *you* are her roommate." The way he said "you" heightened Liz' color. She kept looking at him, Holly thought, the way these girls all gazed at pictures of their favorite movie idols.

Holly was becoming embarrassed at Liz's evident "crush." She was actually speechless for a minute. "Shoot!" Holly said under her breath. "She's as dead a duck as I was when I first met Ted. Did I look that idiotic when I first ran into *him?* Let's hope not."

Mentally chewing her fingernails, Holly stood by nervously until Liz recovered and began to talk with Jack. Finally she and Ted offered their hands in a parting gesture and made prodigious offers of their hospitality.

She heard Liz say, "You must join us for part of the holidays. Holly too, of course." Then Liz flew over and threw an arm around her.

Jack was enthusiastic. "A real ski-lodge? In the arctic wilds of our vast state? Oh, boy. That sounds super. What say, Holly? Want to go?"

A glance at Holly's face changed his mind instantly. "What am I thinking of?" He stepped beside Holly and took her hand. "This girl wants to see her folks. After all, it's Christmas. We'll take a rain check on that, though. Thanks, Ted. Good to meet you — and your sister." His voice dropped to a reverent low as he spoke the last word and Liz looked as though her world had suddenly collapsed. She shot him a soulful look, climbed into the red convertible, glanced enviously at Holly, and they were off.

Holly had a mental flash-back of Jack's play acting in the high school back home. He and Ted were both smooth talkers, she concluded. But she was positive that Jack's "line" was from the salesman's angle rather than a playboy's. This was a comfort to her, personally. She was confident that Jack was not as interested in the acquaintance of Liz as in her mention of the plate glass windows of their lodge.

She smiled when Jack said, "Wow, Hol. Did you hear that?" He opened the door and helped her into the car. "Talk about a prospect for glass! Those Hollisters are going to hear from me."

Holly laughed aloud and settled back to enjoy her big holiday. She liked the way Jack drove; he didn't spin the tires on his take-off like the college fellows but took a steady pace through the town. She was surprised when he pulled to the curb before a drug store.

"You have a girl friend in there," he said. "Guess who is in there shopping right now. Janet and my brother, Billy the kid. Picked 'em both up at that crummy Bible school in Chi. What they see in that place I can't. But skip it. We only have a minute to talk alone. Holly, I'm going places with this Patterson Company. I've got the world around my little finger. The old bank account is soaring and I have everything a man wishes for in life except the most important—"

"You're so right, Jack," she said quickly, ready to tell him what Christ meant to her.

He clasped her hand. "Honey, you've just got to give me a break. Let's talk and talk some more this weekend together. I have to report in the Chi office at eight bells Monday morning. Big deal coming up. But I want to go back with a light heart. Not this lonely ache. Holly, you know I've always loved you—"

They were interrupted by the doors opening and Janet's greeting, "Isn't this great fun, Holly? All of us going home for Christmas!"

And Bill's grave but friendly, "Good to see you again, Holly."

19

The spell was broken, but the yearning in Jack's eyes and the urgency in his appeal touched chords of memory which had not been stirred for some time. Holly's experience with Ted brought Jack into clearer focus. She was even more shaken in her resolves when he told them, "I've given up smoking, Bill — Jan — Holly. What say to that, folks?"

"I've said before and I shall say again — " Bill began when Jack broke in.

"I know, Billy Sunday. I need Christ in my life. Well, I'm not saying I don't. In fact, I've decided to start going to church. All I need is a sweet good partner in life who will keep me on the straight and narrow." He glanced sidewise at Holly who wrinkled her nose in mock displeasure.

"Janet, what you been doing? Exams this week?" She turned to face her friends, thankful for their presence in the car.

Their conversation made the trip go fast. While each one told experiences of the past weeks, Holly noticed a difference in Jack; he was mature for his age; gone was the rash youth. The ride was delightful and Holly grew more relaxed and contented with every passing hour.

She was almost disappointed when they pulled into her driveway in Dayton and Jack said, "Can't see you till Friday night at the church program, Holly. Big deal the company needs me to cover. Will it be all right if I stop for you then?"

As Jo Ann and Timmy ran to the car and Bill jumped out with her luggage, Holly unconsciously returned the quick pressure of Jack's handshake. It was hard to keep her inner longings from showing when he looked at her that way. He was interpreting her response as acquiescence. Should she start going with him again? Couldn't she lead him to Christ by dating and having more opportunity of talking with him? He seemed to depend on her. As he walked with her to the door she tried to think of an answer.

He whispered, "Sweetheart, please, say yes. You know that I love you."

And Holly knew he meant every word he said. He wasn't Ted Hollister.

"I'll see you at church, Jack," she said unsteadily. "We'll talk there — afterward. I think they are having a party somewhere. We'll see."

She waved as they drove off to take Janet home. Then Jo Ann and Timmy claimed her.

Home was a haven of rest for her, and Holly, relaxing from strains of the past weeks, sang as she went about the house.

"Seems like old times when you were here in Dayton High," her mother remarked.

Timmy followed his big sister for two days, asking her questions about the fabulous ski lodge, her rich "friends," and the big city of Chicago. He did this when he could manage to be alone with her for a few minutes, for their parents frowned on his asking personal questions.

"Ya know that big guy who talked to Dad like he was a dumb country preacher who'd never been ta school? With that nutty dame who snapped the whip and acted like this guy was her butler — like in plays — ya know who I mean?" Timmy said all in one breath. He was watching Holly set the table and knew their mother would soon be back from the store with Jo Ann.

Holly smiled in recognition. "Your descriptions are quite adequate. I think you mean Gregory Baines, the son of the renowned Dr. Bruce Baines in Chicago."

"Yeah. That's the one. D'ya know what? This Greg guy came to see Dad in his office and he didn't act like that other time. His face was different. And after he left and we were eatin' supper and Dad prayed at table first — he had to quit prayin' cause he got all choked up and we all waited till he whispered, 'You all go ahead.' Then he told us he felt awful for Greg. He said the guy said he was lost and couldn't find his way. Boy! Dad said Greg's dad was rich and famous and had done a big sin that kept his own son from ris — ris — what's the word, Hol?"

"Respect?"

"Yeah! From respecting and loving his own father. So Greg can't go home for Christmas. He's lost somewhere. No one to go home to."

A banging at the back door sent Timmy skipping to answer, and Holly ran for her coat. Trembling, she ran down the street to the church and straight to her father's study.

Len Wilson, the high school teacher, was talking with the pastor at his door and welcomed her heartily.

89

"Holly, it's wonderful to see you young people back in town for awhile. Our college and business age group shrinks to nothing when you are all away. Don't forget the big party at our house next Monday night. It's after Christmas and all the young people, senior high as well as college age, are coming. We're planning a big time."

"That will be grand, Mr. Wilson. It's so good to be home. It seems more like home each time I return."

After their friend left, Pastor McRae said, "What is it, honey?" And, noting her expression, he closed the door after them.

"Dad, I'm worried about Gregory Baines. I've simply got to talk to you about him."

"Sit down." Her father indicated a leather chair and he sat at his desk.

She wondered what first to say.

"How much of his trouble did he tell you, Dad? Did he tell you — everything — "

"I'm quite positive he told me his life story in full. I am certain that his mother was a born-again Christian and that she was mistreated because of this fact. Gregory concluded — as did I — that his father revealed his guilt in his violent reaction to Sheila's words. Gregory told me all about Sheila, your talk with him in the car on the way back from Chicago, and — other things that were on his mind — I cannot tell you now. We'll see how God leads first. The part I have told you is what you already knew.

"Gregory is, of course, completely uprooted. His faith in the modernist's viewpoint of sin and God's remedy has been torn apart before his eyes. He now believes that sin is black and hideous and he told me that he now fears sin. He fears what it can do to a person's heart and life. But it is impossible for him to discuss the Bible with me — and his own need — when his mind is so engrossed with these recent events. The father he was reared to follow, led him into quicksand and he is even now struggling to escape."

Pastor McRae pushed back his chair and paced the floor. "I tried to lead him to the Lord; I showed him the Scripture about Christ, the only foundation for our faith, and that all other ground is sinking sand. He is so burdened with trouble that he cannot comprehend my message.

"And Holly — one thing I can tell you — he seems to feel personally responsible for dragging you into his troubles. That was the way he expressed it."

"Why, it wasn't his fault," Holly cried. "He didn't know it would turn out that way — he had no idea — "

Her father watched her calmly. "I told him not to feel that way. I knew he could not help the circumstances. But he mentioned that it was his fault in the first place for your accident up north."

Holly blushed. She had not written the full particulars. She looked down at her hands. "He shouldn't feel that way. I'll tell him so when I see him again. Oh Dad! He was completely broken up. I hardly knew what to say in the car on that last trip — but I talked to him about God and His love — and he seemed to listen for awhile — "

The phone rang, jarring their thoughts.

"It's Mother," he announced. "She wondered where you were and wants us home for dinner."

They walked home in silence. Suddenly, before they entered the side door, her father paused with a hand on her arm.

"One more thing. You needn't let on to the folks here — it might worry your mother — but you might give this some thought. At least, I think you should be on guard; Gregory seemed to fear for your safety. Said his father was desperate and would stop at nothing to keep his reputation, and that Sheila too would stop at nothing to extricate herself from his accusations. You see, Holly, you are the pawn in the middle of this game. But we'll talk more later."

Timmy's face at the door brought them back to the present. Holly tried to recapture the holiday mood; it wouldn't do for her family to sense something wrong.

She could hardly wait for a moment to be alone; she wanted to think over her father's last remarks. But Jo Ann and Mother were full of plans for more Christmas shopping and she entered their discussions. Prayer meeting took an hour and something she heard after church sent her thoughts reeling in another direction.

20

Leaving church, Janet clasped Holly's arm. "I'm so happy tonight. Aren't you, Holly?"

They stood on the steps of the church and breathed the icy air. The snow glittered like a blanket of sequins in the glow from lighted windows.

"When we get a few minutes to talk privately, I'll have to tell you some things. Mainly because I value your prayers."

At Holly's strained undertone, Janet peered into her friend's face. Bill's call turned their faces toward the door.

"Hi there, girls. Want a ride tonight, Janet?"

Even as Janet nodded, an elderly man called from one of the parked cars, "Wait there, young man. I want to see you," and shuffled over to them.

He shook hands with all three and proceeded to talk.

"Good to see you back, Bill. We're mighty proud of you. You confessed Christ as your Saviour here at church and I see you are following His leading. Just wanted to say that we'll have to keep praying for your brother, Jack.

"My wife and I were dining at the Smorgasbord up the expressway and there, across from us in that ante-room they save for big parties, was a table of men and women all dressed up. Looked like a big celebration or something. And we saw Jack sitting with them and blowing smoke rings into the air with the rest of that ungodly crowd. My, My! — How that boy has changed since he left Dayton. Only a year and he has that worldly air about him — you'd think he was in his late twenties.

"My wife and I said, 'Look at the difference in two brothers.' Now, Bill, you both sat under the sound of the Gospel. Jack heard it straight from Pastor the same as you."

"Yes," Bill agreed, smiling pleasantly.

"Now I know it is none of my business, Bill. Just couldn't help but tell you what we noticed. You know how we are here in church—just one big interested family. Things like this about Jack we only mention as a reason for more prayer. We'll be praying more than ever now, that he'll accept salvation."

Janet and Holly looked at each other. When their friend left, Bill said, "So he's given up smoking. Only around you, Holly. I've heard Jack say more than once that a man cannot succeed in selling unless he goes along with the crowd. Well, let's not give up. Let's pray definitely that he'll see his need of the Lord."

"Yes," said Janet. "And Holly, how is Gregory Baines? Have you had any more talks with him about his need of Christ?"

"Oh, yes." Holly hesitated, wondering what not to say. Then she smiled brightly. "Oh, yes, Jan. And guess what! The other day he asked me to sing 'How Great Thou Art.' Remember, you sang it that evening in Chicago? In his apartment? He didn't forget you. He mentions you every time we are together. Your testimony made a real impact. Do pray for him too."

She waved good-by and walked slowly toward the parsonage. So Jack had failed to keep his word; he lacked strength of purpose to do what he knew was right. One thing she knew: it was not strength of character he lacked. Jack was not a Ted Hollister. He meant what he said; he simply lacked the power—which power he could have—if he would accept the salvation God offered.

Beneath the Christmas cheer at home, Holly felt a deep grief for Greg in his sorrow and wondered at her disappointment in Jack. Why had she become so involved with Jack Martin? Bill was her own age; it was Janet and Bill and she who had "skipped rope together" as Jack mentioned in Chicago. But then, Jack had always exaggerated. He was an inveterate actor.

Even at the church program Friday evening, Jack's entrance in the church foyer created a cosmopolitan atmosphere. Her frustration prevented Holly from enjoying his company.

She remembered how thrilled she had been when he first "noticed" her. He was two grades ahead of her and had not known she existed until she was a Junior in high school. Then he had fairly "rushed her." Since he had been the idol of the school, their best actor in the senior plays, and known as "a lion among ladies," Holly had fallen in love with him. *He was the start of my desire to see more of life. Well, you've seen enough to last awhile, Holly McRae.*

What made him look so much older? She noticed the fine lines around his eyes. She smiled but knew she lacked confidence in him. How could a girl know for sure when she met the right one? She couldn't help but like Jack. Was it possible to win him to Christ by dating him? She knew what Janet would say. She'd quote that verse about light and darkness and not being unequally yoked together with unbelievers.

When they were seated for the Christmas program, Holly turned to the passage in Second Corinthians and pointed it out to Jack. He took one glance, nodded his head absently and whispered, "When can we be alone? I haven't had a chance to see you without someone around."

"Why don't you come over to Eagan's tonight? Didn't Bill tell you? We're all invited to the singspiration."

His look of impatience held a tinge of repugnance. "It's you I'm interested in," he shot back.

They stood with the congregation to sing, "Hark, the Herald Angels Sing." When the lights dimmed for the program, Jack stirred uneasily. He changed positions several times. After a few minutes he whispered, "I'll be back. Forgot to make a long distance phone call." He patted her hand and slipped out to a side exit.

The call seemed to last half an hour. Holly tried to shake a feeling of depression. She pushed back the clammy thought but it kept protruding. She tried to concentrate on the children's voices up front.

"And there were in the same country shepherds abiding in the field . . . *It's too late. Your opportunity for witness is gone.* The shepherds filed on stage from behind the choir loft and a bright light shined from the ceiling. *I'll talk to Jack tonight.* She tried to relax.

When Jack returned to her side the program had advanced to the high school age choir. The Nativity scene was lifted to its ultimate goal, the gospel story. Parts of the "Messiah" were sung. Holly was glad the program ended so triumphantly with everyone singing his best. It made an impact on several visitors. At Pastor McRae's invitation, three adults walked to the front of the church to confess Christ as their Lord and Saviour.

As people crowded into the foyer after the service, Holly could hardly believe her eyes when she saw Jack's mother approaching them. Mrs. Martin was a heavy-set lady, impressive in rich furs and flashing jewels.

She arranged a smile especially for Holly and said affectedly, "My deah, your program was simply divine. I shall have to rush away; my club is meeting for a snack at the Rendezvous. Bye, bye, Jackie." Her voice lowered as she leaned toward her son, but Holly heard her words: "And, honey, after you get through with Billy's little friends — it will still be early for *us* — come by. There's someone I want you to meet."

The way she said "someone" and flickered her eyes toward Holly was unmistakable. Jack patted his mother's arm. "See ya, Mother. But don't get any ideas. I have some of my own."

She looked petulant. "I hope they're not like Billy's!" She tossed her head, pulled her furs closer to her throat, and hurried out.

Jack followed Holly outside. "She's afraid of this church and its influence over me," he grinned.

"Well?"

"Well, after *all,* Holly. You've been around a *little* bit. Surely you can see there is more to life than the narrow sphere we have known in this town."

"Sure." She stepped into his car. He closed the door and hurried around to the driver's side.

"I know who she wants me to meet," he said. "A high flyer from the east — millionaire's daughter. Holly, money doesn't mean as much to me as it does to my mother. Believe me. Not *that* much. Holly, I'm telling you the truth. You are the only girl for me. You're the one girl in the whole world who means anything — everything — to me. I want you to marry me. I can give you anything you'd ever want — I'll do anything you want — I'll be anything you want. I've been in love with you ever since we ran into each other at that ball game two years ago. Remember?"

"That was two years ago!" She trembled as from a chill. His words about love and marriage were tempting.

Seeing more church folk coming to their cars, Jack pulled out of the lot and drove slowly down the street toward Janet's house. Under a street light he stopped by the curb. Cars were parked in the Eagan's driveway. They sat looking out, the car motor humming in monotone.

Then he took her hand and leaned close to her. "Can you honestly say that your love for me hasn't lasted? I still love you. Will you marry me?"

A shadow fell across her heart. The cross. And the memory of an anguished soul over the tragic death of a Christian mother. A supernatural strength lifted her above the temptation to yield.

"I am a Christian, Jack. Unless you turn yourself over to Christ, I cannot talk with you any more about it."

She felt the stab of separation when he released the hand clasp. His sad look penetrated her soul and his dark eyes reproached her.

In a low voice he said slowly, "Why didn't you talk like this a long time ago? It might have helped — then. I liked to hear your father preach — but — I thought you weren't 'sold' on all this." He gestured toward Janet's house. "I've had a taste of a different life from this. And I like it. I'm in the money and I like that.

"Holly, you know how you used to holler about being a poor preacher's kid. I wouldn't remind you, darling, only I want you to know why I've a certain goal in mind. Look at me, Holly. We can enjoy life together. I promise you I'll go to church with you — anything — but I can't turn my life over to — this — as you and Bill have — not yet. But dearest, I promise you that I'll think about it. *I promise.* Will you think about me? And let me know when you change your mind?"

"Don't wait for me, Jack. I'll not change my mind."

He interpreted the tears in her voice and eyes as a response to his love. It was the futility of their relationship that shook her. And the knowledge that her worldiness in high school days had kept him from coming to Christ. When he suddenly took her into his arms she cried out: "I mean it. I'm sorry; but I can't."

Before she should yield to his will, Holly flung open the car door and jumped out. He called after her, "I'll wait for you, Holly."

21

In no mood to join the singspiration, Holly paused by the Eagan's door until Jack drove on; then she hurried down the street toward home. A vision of Liz looking back at her in obvious envy passed before her eyes. Liz would really think she was crazy if she knew this! Turning down the offer of a man like Jack! A big wedding of the kind girls dreamed. A church wedding.

But the mental picture of it didn't quite focus. Her father would not officiate, of course. She had heard him turn down such weddings before; he refused to unite a believer with an unbeliever.

She lifted her eyes to the stars and took a deep breath of the frosty air. Somewhere in the sub-conscious she knew someone else who walked alone tonight. She groped for the connection and a song flashed through her mind. "Somebody cares when your heart aches . . . "

It was Greg. It was his loneliness which overshadowed her own. Greg — without God, whose love and care could lift him above the burden — was "lost somewhere." As Timmy said, he had no one to go home to. Holly thought of her dear family at the parsonage: their loving exchange of gifts around the Christmas tree; their singing together around the piano; their fellowship at dinner, at breakfast, and in between.

Surely I am not turning away from the kind of love I want. Real love, to be completely satisfying, has to originate in God.

"All other love is centered in self," she explained to Janet later.

They had agreed to help Pastor McRae fold papers for mailing. It was Monday, the day after Christmas, when Holly finally had opportunity to confide in her friend. She related the strange events of the past weeks while they sat together at a long table, folding letters.

Janet listened with interest. "You'll never regret this decision about Jack, Holly. I know how hard it must be to — to say no — but we'll keep praying for him."

"I'm afraid it is too late to do that," Holly said dully.

Janet looked her concern. "Do you really love Jack?"

"I'm all mixed up. I'd marry him — I know I would — if he were right with God. But even then, I'm not at all sure. How can you know if you've met the right one?"

Her father, entering the office from his study, stopped short. "I can answer that one," he laughed. "There won't be any doubt about it."

"You know," Janet laughed with him, "he's right. You will know, Holly. Beyond the shadow of a doubt."

The burden lifted. Holly felt God's peace surpassing the sadness. Her heartache eased; a song lifted her spirit; she began to hum at her work.

"Going to skate awhile this after?" Janet asked, standing up to stack a pile of papers.

"Guess not. Wilsons' pond will be full of kids. They've invited the senior high department, you know. I'll wait till after their dog roast. Even then — with no date — "

"This isn't merely a time for dates, Holly. Ride over with me. Bill has to pick up some visitors from Milwaukee; Len and Dot told me yesterday at church that we're in for a real musical treat tonight. Some young man who sings — forget his name — a recording artist the Wilsons know."

"Sounds wonderful. We need something like this, don't we, Jan? The fellowship of other Christian young people. Right now I can testify that it really helps. And Wilsons' gorgeous ranch-style home has been dedicated to the Lord. I hope some day — "

"So do I," Janet breathed, as Holly paused in her dreams.

They both broke out laughing as they guessed each other's thoughts.

Janet passed by the window and exclaimed, "Someone's driving up to the study door, Pastor. Who in your church drives a white Cadillac? Holly! Do you suppose — "

Holly scrambled to her feet and ran to look. It was Greg. They both hurried back to their work lest he should find them at the window. Pastor McRae heard from his study and came out. The office door opened and Greg stepped inside. Holly started. His face was haggard. Her father held out both hands. The two stood silently for a moment until Greg could speak.

She loved her father for saying quietly, "You've had a rough time, son. Here, sit down."

Janet nudged Holly and they hurried into their wraps. Greg looked up dully, one hand to his forehead. His eyes met theirs and he started to rise.

"Don't go — Holly — Janet — you are my — friends." His voice broke. He sat forward with his face in his hands.

They knew he was desperately tired. The girls quietly sat down and waited. Holly glanced at Janet and saw tears in her eyes. Their hearts ached for him. Pastor McRae pulled a chair beside Greg and waited for him to speak.

Greg lifted his head from his hands and looked at the pastor. "He admitted it. I called him on it and he practically boasted that he—in his words—'did what was best for her.' I was so unnerved I shouted at him: 'You mean that you had nothing more to prove my mother's insanity than her belief in God and Christ—her prayer life?' And he flew into such a rage I thought he would have a heart attack.

"He said after all the years he'd schooled me on the powers of the mind—was I going to stoop to imbibing the opiate of the poor devils who needed something to bolster a faulty ego. He called me a 'stupid son of my religious fanatic of a mother,' said he'd inquired about the plebeian preacher who—" Greg glanced apologetically at Holly—"whose daughter I brought home. I'm sorry, Holly. I didn't mean to burden you dear people with all this—"

He broke off abruptly and buried his face in his hands.

Pastor McRae laid a hand on his shoulder and prayed aloud: "Father, God, Thou hast told us in Thy Word to pour out our hearts before Thee; Thou art a refuge for us. Help Gregory to pour out his troubles without fear; lift the weight from his soul and give him clear understanding. In Jesus' name we ask this, Amen."

When Greg lifted his face, it was wet with tears but the gray shade had lifted; color came into his face and he spoke with more freedom.

"I told him plainly that the knowledge of what he did to my mother was all I needed to convince me that his philosophy was dead wrong. I told him I had come to believe in the fact of God—and what the Bible said about sin—"

Here Greg stood shakily and faced them. Two bright spots appeared on his cheek bones. The pupils of his eyes dilated as he recalled the scene with his father.

"He picked up a thick book and hurled it. It caught me on the shoulder; I opened the door to leave and he literally yelled at me." Greg sat down dazedly; his shoulders sagged. "Something about staying in school until I was educated sufficiently to instruct *him.*"

They knew he had purposely left out much of this last conversation. Holly could imagine what his father had done to him.

"Lila left on the day before Christmas for a trip to Europe. Her nerves, she said in a letter to us. She cleaned out two large banking accounts my father shared with her. She was legally in her rights; but all this put together—Sheila's blackmailing and Strands at his throat with those letters in their possession—all this is catching up with him, Pastor. He is headed for a nervous or physical breakdown or both."

"Greg, I am concerned about *you*. We have been praying for you night and day. Look, son. You have taken the first step toward the salvation God offers you, by acknowledging sin and calling it by its correct name. God's Word declares 'all have sinned.' I have sinned. You have sinned.

"Now look up to Christ Jesus, Son of the living God, who suffered and shed His blood to pay for our sins. God raised Him from the dead; He has all power to save and keep us. If you believe this and receive Him as your Saviour right now you will begin to live — spiritually. God calls it the 'new birth.' You will be born again."

"Yes. I wanted to talk with you about it — soon — " Greg's voice grew faint.

Pastor McRae saw the gray look on his face and said quickly, "Holly, run and prepare a room for him. He needs rest or he'll be ill."

The girls rushed out, Holly again meeting his eyes. His hopeless expression puzzled her. Greg had never before looked at her like that. *He seems to think I am blaming him for some of this.*

She was glad for Janet's help. Mother McRae went to work in the kitchen to prepare hot soup for the traveler. Timmy shouted for joy when they said he could spend the night with his friends.

The girls cleaned Timmy's room, pulled the shades against the bright sunlight, and left Timmy's Bible on the bedside table.

"When he awakes, he's sure to open it," said Janet. "I'm going to pray that he will receive Christ today. No later than midnight."

They looked at each other. The party! Christian fellowship!

"Let's do!" they both spoke at once. Then the girls broke into hysterical giggles.

Rushing downstairs, they ran into Holly's mother. Janet explained, "We're always getting the same idea at the same time."

Holly hugged her mother in a sudden affectionate embrace. "We'll take him to Wilson's tonight. It will do him more good than anything."

Janet cried, "Holly! He loves organ music!"

Even Mrs. McRae became enthusiastic and joined their mood. She patted them on the head and said, "Let's all keep quiet then, so he can get some sleep. I think this is a grand idea — to take him with you tonight."

They were thinking of the Wilson's electric organ in their spacious living room. Holly could picture the logs burning in their long fire-place, the picture window overlooking a little lake, and their friends gathered in groups, playing games or visiting.

The girls spent the afternoon at Janet's house and returned to Holly's for the evening meal. Mother McRae delayed dinner to give Greg more time for sleep.

Jo Ann turned on the record player. "Greg should like this," she said to Holly. "The 'duo-magic' of some Christian artists at the keyboard. Man, can they play like crazy!"

22

The table was set with Christmas candles, holly berries for decoration, and their best china.

"You think of everything, Moms," Holly whispered, kissing her mother on one ear.

Janet carried more chairs to the table. "This looks so cheerful; just think what a horrible Christmas Greg had!"

Finally he appeared. His look of appreciation warmed their hearts. Everyone was seated and Pastor McRae thanked God for the food.

Greg looked across the table at the girls. "You are so privileged to have a home — and parents — like yours. No amount of money can give one peace and contentment such as this. Education is fine — but fruitless if it does not produce results such as this — your wonderful home life."

Pastor smiled. "Gregory, that is precisely what the Bible tells us: 'godliness with contentment is great gain, for we brought nothing into this world, and it is certain we can carry nothing out . . .'"

"Considering the law of cause and effect," Greg went on, "brings me to the conclusion that your Christian home is the direct result of contact with Christ. Am I right?"

Everyone at the table came to life; several spoke out at once, but he could hear "yes" on all sides.

After the lively discussion Greg turned to Janet. "When does your spring term begin at LaSalle?"

Janet was radiant. "You have plenty of time to enroll, Greg. The middle of January."

Everyone laughed as she took for granted his desire to change schools.

"I'm in earnest," he said smiling. "I'm ready to put this thing to the test. If the Bible is actually the Word of God — as you folk say — then I want to study it and know for myself. I'll confess; I can't help but see the result of your faith. I need the assurance you have

— the power to live as—'' he stopped, glanced at Holly, then looked down at his plate.

He turned to the pastor. "This will be the final link that will break all connection with my father. He is likely to try something— but never mind that. One thing I can be thankful for: he is powerless to touch my trust fund which provides for my education. There is sufficient to cover my expenses for a period of years if I am careful.

"My first move in economy involves transportation. I shall appreciate your advice on these matters, Pastor.''

Holly's father told her later: "I like that boy's reasoning. He is sensible for his years. I believe he would make a fine teacher of young people, like Len Wilson.''

"Yes, and won't he like the Wilsons? All of this put together is leading him to the Lord. I'm so thrilled.'' Holly's eyes sparkled, then clouded.

Her father looked at her intently. "What's the matter?''

"Nothing.''

He paused a moment. Then she confessed: "Dad, Greg and I were getting to be such close friends. But now—since he came this time—he seems to avoid me. He talks more with Janet. Oh, don't get me wrong,'' she went on quickly. "It's not that—only—oh, well, that is exactly what I wanted. I kept telling her they had everything in common. Their love of music—''

Timmy ran up to them and whispered loudly, "Ya know what, Hol? He's in there looking at all the records and asking Janet all kinds of questions. Boy! He's a lot different this time. I like him. Don't you?''

Jo Ann waved her sister out of the kitchen. "My turn tonight, sis. Jan says to get crackin' or you'll never make Wilsons'.''

Holly felt a strangeness between them when she and Greg went out to the car. Janet wanted to drive; Greg opened the door for Holly, then sat beside her in the front seat.

"I'll never forget the miserable time you had in my car on that trip north.'' His low voice was meant for her ears alone.

Holly glanced at him. He was looking down. She said, "It wasn't your fault, Greg. Nothing that happened that weekend was your fault.''

His eyes met hers; she was startled at his expression. She felt a glow of comfort. They had shared some unusual experiences which drew them together; but she must not forget that he was turning more and more to Janet. They would make a wonderful couple.

Seeing Wilsons' home through Gregory's eyes gave Holly a new thrill. Everything was perfect; it was exactly as she had pictured it. Len and Dot greeted them cordially and introduced Greg to everyone.

Len explained: "We call our college and business age group the C and B'ers. We're about to choose two teams here for our first game, 'Password.' Here, Janet, you take that side and Holly can sit here with her friend, Gregory Baines.

"Bill, you take the lead while I step downstairs and see how things are going with the seniors at ping-pong and carroms."

Holly settled back in the luxurious couch and looked at Greg. His face mirrored his interest; she saw a look of admiration when he surveyed their surroundings: the animated young people, the lovely furnishings of Wilson's colonial-style home, and the cheery crackling of logs on the hearth.

Bill was showing a piece of paper to his team. He explained to Greg and other new ones: "We have one word, a noun. Each of us will give your side a one-word clue. You must guess our word. Go ahead, team."

The girl opposite Greg said, "Hands."

Greg guessed, "Gloves?"

The boy next in line said, "face."

Holly answered, "Soap?"

Someone down the line cried, "Is it 'clock'?"

"No fair, it wasn't your turn. Yes, our word was 'clock.' Now you get the idea of how to play the game, we'll think up another word for you."

Holly's side shouted, "No, you don't! It's our turn." And the evening was off to a good start.

Greg's interest in the game brought him to life. Holly sensed the change and was radiant. She smiled across to Janet knowing that she, too, noticed Greg's lift of spirit. As always, the game progressed with accelerated hilarity.

Greg laughed with them and said to Holly, "I've never had so much fun at a party." Later he told her and Janet together, "This is what I call a good time. It is completely relaxing."

After an hour, the C and B'ers traded places with the high schoolers and played action games in the basement recreation room. Another fire was burning there.

In the fellowship of her Christian friends, Holly's baffling problems melted into the background and this charmed evening took the center of the stage. She wished it could go on and on. Bill and Greg doubled with Janet and her at ping pong. She was surprised at Greg's agility. As the games progressed, he and Bill seemed to click; they were soon talking together like old buddies.

When the Wilsons served refreshments at the fireside table, Greg and Bill stood in a corner with their trays, talking for half an hour longer.

Janet, passing by Holly, remarked: "I'll bet Greg asked him about

LaSalle. Isn't it simply grand for Greg to have this happy evening after the cruel experience in his home?''

"I'll say," Holly answered. "He begins to look more like himself."

Len Wilson called for them to join the group upstairs for some music. Janet was marshaled to the piano and Dot Wilson to the organ. A young man led them in familiar songs and choruses.

Holly sat opposite Bill and Greg and couldn't help but notice Greg's appreciation of their music. He didn't know the words but often closed his eyes, rested his head on the high back of his chair, and looked contented.

"Rolled away, rolled away . . . every burden of my heart rolled away." Holly sang joyfully, realizing more fully what these songs meant to many a young person in the room.

When they were asked for their favorite songs, Greg suggested, "How Great Thou Art." The song leader motioned a tall, blond fellow to his side and announced: "We have a distinguished guest with us. Len asked him to sing especially for you tonight. He is on his way east and stopped by to see his friends, the Wilsons. Bob, would you sing this one for us — at least two verses — and we'll join you on the chorus."

A deep quiet settled over the crowd when Bob began to sing. Some recognized the voice they had heard on radio and records.

Two other requests followed Greg's. When he sang, "I am amazed that God should ever love me . . . so full of sin . . . " Holly and Greg looked at each other, remembering an evening in Chicago when Janet played and sang. The words seemed to stir Greg deeply. Holly closed her eyes when she noticed his battle with emotion.

She felt the tears aching in her own throat as she remembered his heartache and her own grief over sins of the past. The old weight clamped down; she remembered in a rush of remorse how she had failed to influence Jack for Christ. Would he ever come to the Lord, now that his one burning ambition in life was to reach the peak in the selling business?

Then Holly's heart stood still. She was entirely conscious of Greg's need as Bob sang, "I never walk alone, Christ walks beside me. He is the dearest Friend I'll ever know . . . "

A glance at Greg showed him leaning forward, his face in his hands. Bill put one arm around him; Greg found a handkerchief and again covered his face. He wasn't the only one moved by the song. Its message touched more than one heart.

Len Wilson talked briefly of God's love and provision for His children. He asked for testimonies and many of the young people told what God had done for them in the past year. Some told what

God meant to them as they attended godless colleges and walked among unbelievers.

Greg listened intently, unmindful of his brimming eyes and the handkerchief in his hands.

No one wanted to leave. After the testimonies, some lingered by the fireside, talking in subdued tones. Some crowded around Bob, begging him for "one more song." Len joined Bill in a discussion with Greg, and the girls wandered about the long room, talking with first one, then another. It was midnight when the party broke up.

Greg's last comment that night thrilled the McRae family.

"I am sure that God spoke to me this night. He is real. And I want to be a Christian."

23

When it was arranged that Bill would ride to Chicago with Greg and show him around the Bible Institute, Janet decided to catch a ride at the same time.

"It will save train fare," she said, "and is so much easier to transport my things. We'll help on the gas, Greg."

"Don't mention it." He smiled at her. "I owe you people a debt of gratitude I'll never be able to repay." Greg turned to Holly and she had difficulty swallowing a lump in her throat.

When he saw that she was unable to speak, Greg clasped her hands firmly. "Holly, my precious friend, I shall never forget it was you who brought me to see my need of God. Your father tells me I can't understand the Bible until I receive Christ as my Saviour and I have His Spirit to guide me."

He kept Holly's hands in his and looked over at the pastor. "So I'll ask you to keep praying for me. I want to have this life you are telling me about. Truly I do. May I come to see you again and talk more about it?" He pressed her hands harder, then released them suddenly.

Her father stepped forward to shake hands and assured Greg: "We want you to come every weekend it is possible for you to get away. And we are confident that God will answer our prayers—both yours and ours."

When Greg saw tears in Mrs. McRae's eyes, he bent quickly and kissed her.

"I'll not say good-by, son," she said. "We want you to come and go like one of the family."

It was Greg's turn to swallow hard. He shook hands gravely with Jo Ann, punched Timmy lightly, winked at him as though they shared a secret, and hurried outside to the car.

Holly waved to them as they backed down the driveway; then she ran upstairs. A gray, stormy sky darkened her room; she opened and closed dresser drawers, rearranged clothes hangers, got out her travel case and inspected it.

Finally she sat down and stared at the bleak sky. What was there to look forward to? She had never in her life felt so utterly lonely. Her best friends were enjoying fellowship in that car and would enjoy being together often, from now on.

She slowly descended the stairs. There were dishes to do. She would help Jo Ann make her new jumper. She must not let her family know that she missed — was it *Greg* she missed? For the first time it occurred to Holly that she was suffering more from a casual separation from this new friend than she had felt from saying no to Jack's proposal.

Between conversations with her family, Holly found herself thinking more and more about Gregory Baines. The way he looked at her on different occasions. The way her family took him to its heart. The way he joined in the fun at Wilson's party. *Jack would have been bored.*

It was with reluctance that she left the home town for her second term at State U. Life became meaningless. When she arrived this time, the university was shorn of its magic. A sudden thaw waved an invisible wand and the snowy white campus turned drab gray. Ugly rivulets of dirty water dripped down the lawns into the street.

Holly climbed the flights of stairs in her dorm, flung her cases on the bed, and sighed audibly. Liz would arrive at the last minute, probably in the morning for classes.

Holly tried to shake a feeling of depression. Nothing shook it loose; even the friendly chatter of the girls on her floor didn't help. There was simply nothing cheerful to look forward to. She sat down at the mirror and looked bleakly at her own countenance. "What's the matter with you?" she said. "Cheer up. Count your many blessings." Then she flopped on the bed and tried not to think.

Just before lights-out bell, Liz stormed in.

"Of all the dumb rules! They have nerve to tell me!" she panted. "They won't even let Jack carry my cases to the top of the stairs! Afraid he'll see some girls!" She swore and looked at Holly. "Run down. He wants to say something to you—what for, I'm sure I don't know."

"You mean Jack Martin?" Holly was incredulous.

"Who else?" Liz snapped.

Holly ran.

He was standing in the hall looking up. She took in the sporty jacket and cap and felt her smile erasing.

His first words disarmed her. "Will you marry me, Holly? I'm still waiting. And don't get me wrong. I'm not Liz's date. Just gave her and her gang a ride down.

"They called me in Chi to run up for a day and give an estimate on some glass walls for an annex on their lodge. I got the order, honey. Do you know what that means?"

She pulled her hand from his grasp and her eyes snapped. "Yes. Lots of money. Well, that should make you happy. Now please go — and forget me, Jack."

His look of genuine sorrow caught her attention, even as she turned away. He put both arms around her and held her by the shadowy wall.

"I can't forget you," he whispered. His lips brushed her cheek. Once more she yielded to his embrace. It was hard to fight against a love which was tempting. And she believed Jack loved her.

"I want a little dream home in the suburbs," he breathed in her ear, "and you to come home to. Promise me you'll think about me every day and I'll keep my promise about becoming a Christian — the way you want."

She hesitated, then yielded to the yearning of her own heart. It would be so easy to say a final "yes" to Jack. "I'll think about it. I promise," she whispered.

Liz called from the stair landing. They looked up. She was glamorous in gold cloth lounging pajamas that caught light in shimmering waves.

Holly glanced at Jack's face. He gave a quick nod and waved his hand at Liz. "Bye now," he called. "Hope to see you again, Liz. And many thanks for the wonderful day." His voice was cordial and direct. He turned back to Holly. They heard Liz sputter like a snuffed wick. Then she mounted the stairs noisily.

After he left, Holly slowly followed Liz, remorse flooding her soul. She knew it was wrong to yield to his compromise. She should have waited until he could honestly say that he had received Christ as his own personal Saviour before making any promises. If she wasn't careful, he would have her signing on the dotted line and they would be married *before* he became a Christian. *He has already had plenty of time.*

She felt the barb of Liz' jealousy when they were alone.

"You lucky jerk," Liz flung at her. "If Jack Martin ever asks *me* to marry him, *I* won't take the chance of acting cute and coy and hard-to-get. I'll grab him and hang on to him. He told us he's trying to get you to set a date. So whatcha waiting for? A saint in shining armor? Isn't Jack good enough for your puritan ancestors to approve?"

Seeing Liz in such a surly mood, Holly gave a short laugh and went about the business of retiring for the night. Liz kept goading her, trying to get a rise from Holly. It was on the tip of Holly's tongue to say, "Any good-looking man with money would please you and your rich family," but she thought better of it.

On Saturday Holly was homesick. Liz announced she was hopping a plane for a weekend in Colorado where her brother, Ted, and his fiance, Rene, were looking for a home. They were having a big family gathering at one of the finest winter resorts near Denver. Liz wasn't sure if she would get back to State U before the middle of the week. Classes could wait.

Holly decided to spend the full day in study. She would attempt to pull her B average in art class up to an A.

She felt apart from everything worth living for. State U had lost its charm for her; the bleak winter months stretched ahead in an endless road. Professor Anson's subtle sarcasm aimed at discrediting everything concerning Christ and the Bible grew more disgusting with every passing week. The literature on her "required reading" list echoed the nature of his lectures.

Studies in art progressed from the realm of the basics and abstract to one of more concrete in the form of school ballet dancers who posed for her class. At each session the professor's opinions and remarks kept everyone laughing but Holly. She muttered in class: "He hasn't a decent thought in his head."

The daily dregs from the minds of the unregenerated gave her depression of spirit. As the weeks passed, Holly became increasingly dissatisfied with her art course, the university, and her daily existence.

Jack's flowers and letters were frequent. But he only mentioned his success in selling or his plans for their future together. She knew he had been sincere in his promise of becoming a Christian; but he was too busy to think about it right now.

Holly's sleep was broken early each morning. She found herself talking under her breath to God. "It's normal for a girl to respond to a love like Jack's. He will always be kind about my beliefs. He could never be cruel like Greg's father.

"Of course I want a Christian home that is based on the Rock, Christ Jesus. All other ground is sinking sand. That was the downfall of the Baines' marriage. But it wouldn't happen that way to *us.*"

But it could happen some other way. Shifting sand. The words sounded as clearly in her head as though a voice spoke audibly. She tossed and turned. Five o'clock in the morning as usual. And she was so tired of thinking.

Visions of her past association with Jack kept flashing before her: Jack letting her out at Janet's because he didn't enjoy Christian fellowship with the other young people. His restlessness at church. It would be no different after they were married; that was for sure. *What fellowship hath light with darkness?*

She remembered Greg sitting in the Wilson's home with evident appreciation of their Christian fellowship. It wouldn't be long until he would come to Christ and experience regeneration. Then he and Janet would soon discover how fine a couple they would make. If only Holly could feel about Jack as she did about Greg. *How do I feel about Greg?*

She tried to think it through. Always he had given her the warm glow of gladness as he came near. He was like a friendly big brother. Their friendship was based on a mutual understanding of each other.

From the first meeting, he had responded to conversation about God; he had not tried to avoid the subject. And the more he became interested in spiritual things, the more she had looked forward to seeing him. *I miss him more than I do Jack.*

The bald fact propelled Holly to a sitting position. The bed lurched and squeaked; the campus clock tolled six.

Liz grumbled: "Hol, for cat's sake quit your prowling at all hours of the night. I'm beat!"

24

Three weeks passed before she received Greg's letter. Holly eagerly read the pages while she was in the library.

"My precious friend, Holly," he wrote. "I have taken a tremendous step; you might call it faith. I have quit studies at seminary and am enrolled in North LaSalle. A school that produces such jewels as Janet and Bill can't be far off center.

"My father declares that I've lost my mind, and he would no doubt cause trouble for me here at the Institute if he were not involved in legal battles with the Strands. I'm fearful of the consequences. Would you pray about it for me? Maybe after I have been here this term, I'll learn to pray too. Sincerely yours, with deep appreciation for all you and your dear family have done for me, Greg."

His letter brought a ray of cheer followed by a strange sense of loneliness. Holly felt isolated from friends and loved ones. Greg would soon be taken up with his new and different studies; he would enjoy Bill's friendship and would no doubt see Janet every day. *Such jewels as Janet. Well, that's wonderful. I'll pray for you, dear Greg, and write just one short note in answer to this. And now—back to my studies.*

Final exams were approaching and the pressure mounted. Liz kept needling her about Jack, and Gwen seemed preoccupied. Life at State U was one monotonous dirge.

In the midst of exam week Holly shuffled into her room to find the girls bent over notebooks, their faces glum. She threw her stack of books across the bed and shouted, "Let's relax! We never have any fun around here. I'm throwing a party as of now. Here's a sack of cookies."

Liz snorted; then she yawned, stretched, and smiled at Holly. "For once you have a smart idea, kid. I'll run down to the store for some ice cream. Need the exercise. Be right back. Gwen, what can you bring to the blast?"

Gwen opened a drawer and produced candy bars. Liz waved and left. Holly wondered at the dark smudges around Gwen's eyes. All at once it occurred to her that the tall girl had not been as talkative as usual.

"What's the matter, Gwen? You look beat lately." Holly threw herself on the bed and flipped her sockfeet high on the wall.

Gwen sat down at the mirror and looked at herself. She sat still, chin in hand. She was too quiet for Gwen. Then her eyes met Holly's through the glass.

Holly was startled to see her roommate collapse into sobs. She bounded to the door, closed it, and bent over Gwen. "What is wrong, honey?"

"Everything. Oh, Holly, I wish I had never met Liz Hollister. That party at her fancy lodge has ruined my whole life. Nels rushed me off my feet — I was helpless — the liquor and everything — oh, God in heaven, how can I tell my aunt? She's counting on me. This will nearly kill her."

"Are you sure?" Holly cried.

"Yes, I'm sure. I even saw a doctor."

"Why don't you and Nels get married right away — tell her you want a small wedding at home — or something." Holly hoped she was helping.

Gwen's shoulders shook. She tried to stifle the sobs. When she could speak she cried, "Holly, I don't love him at all. I would never have wanted to marry him. And now I'll have to. But what if he doesn't — "

They both looked at each other in dismay. When Liz breezed in, she saw them sitting gloomily, staring at each other.

"Well of all the gloomsville! What a party atmosphere. Gwen, you never cry! What in the world's going on around here?"

Gwen said, "I'm simply ill, that's all. I find that it will be impossible for me to come back next semester." She looked at Holly warningly.

"Darling!" Liz threw her arms around Gwen. "If it's money — "

Gwen stood up and strode to the window. "Thanks, no, Liz. This is something money can't touch. It's — several other things — circumstances beyond my control — and my aunt's — that's all. I won't talk about it."

The hardness in her voice and the cold look from her eyes sent a chill through Holly. Gwen's cold grief reminded her of Greg's sorrow. Holly felt the impact of tragedy and was shaken.

At semester's end Liz suggested a farewell party for Gwen but Holly did not encourage it. With many other students, Holly and Gwen caught a ride to the train station. They checked Gwen's luggage and stood in a place apart from the crowd to say good-by.

Holly hardly knew where to begin but she knew she must say something. Gwen's heart was too full of grief; she looked hopeless and it frightened Holly.

"Gwen, I — it's hard to tell you this but I've got to — I lived a lie here at State U. If I hadn't, you might have been saved — from this. But Gwen — listen, dear — you can be saved from any more of this kind of sorrow.

"I've got to tell you the truth. I thought I was missing a lot in life by being sheltered in an old-fashioned home. I fell for all that Liz and her crowd had to offer and I, too, came back with a mouthful of sawdust. Gwen, you must write to me.

"I can help you — my father can — to see how much God loves you and how He suffered to set us free from our sins. Christ died to save us. Not merely from the penalty of sin, but from its power, and even from the effects of our sins."

"It's too late." The words sounded brittle as dead leaves crunching underfoot. Gwen's dark-circled eyes showed her agony of spirit.

"It's not too late to start living with Jesus, the Son of God, as your Saviour. Will you write to me — so I can try to explain — I'm terribly sorry, Gwen, but I haven't talked about my faith in Christ. I was ashamed to speak about Him because — you know how it is at school — "

"Yes, kid, I know. We were only interested in dancing. Holly, I am sick of dancing. It was that steady beat — the rhythm — the — oh, I wish I had never gone. Honey — " Gwen's eyes filled. "I'll be so lonesome I'll about die. Just waiting. I'll be glad to hear from you or your father or most anyone, for that matter. Only be sure to keep this a secret between us. No one else in this world knows about it but that devil, Nels, and one angel, you, and — I guess — God."

"You needn't guess about that, dear. You know God knows. And never forget this: He cares. He's proved it by coming down to save us from our sins."

A blast from the speaker announcing her train sent Gwen spinning. She kissed hurriedly, leaving some tears on Holly's face. Gwen waved from the crowd in line at the gate and Holly turned to go, tears dropping from her own eyes.

It was a relief to find a note from Liz saying she would be away for a few days. The same week she heard from Janet.

"Holly, dear, it's only a month until the big Bible Conference here at LaSalle. Could you come down by train or bus for a wonderful weekend? I am so eager to see you; it seems so long since we were home at Christmas. Let me know right away and I'll reserve one of the guest rooms. I do hope you can come. Oh, yes, and Holly! There will be great news for you when you come."

114

25

Holly sent a letter by return mail assuring Janet of her coming. The weeks crept by until the time arrived. She kept wondering about the great news Janet mentioned.

Riding the freeway by bus, Holly thought of the difference in this trip and the ones she had made in Greg's fine car. She wondered what progress he was making in getting acquainted with the Bible and in knowing Jan better.

The Chicago skyline was etched in charcoal smoke from the city. Holly felt the chill in the big lake region. She was uneasy about meeting Jack. He knew she was coming to the city. What would she do with him?

Janet had promised to meet her, for she knew her way around in the subway and elevated trains. When the bus finally pulled into the terminal and the crowd filed out, she saw Jack standing by Janet, his dark eyes searching hers for a sign of response. Holly could only smile warmly at him and wonder at herself for reacting so calmly.

"Holly sweet, Jan says that one of the country's greatest evangelists is in the city this week. I'm going with you girls to hear him. You need protection to and from that district her school is in. What you and Bill ever saw in that place, Jan, I can't fathom.

"Holly, darling, I'm all set for the biggest thrill in the business. They're sending me to Hawaii any time now. Just waiting word from GHQ. If I land that order – one of the biggest hotels in Honolulu – the sky's the limit. Step this way; my car's in the lot."

As they followed, Janet told Holly: "He insisted on meeting you and I insisted that I wanted to meet you too. It's really something! He's been calling every day to ask when you were coming. Oh, Holly! Let's pray that he will yield his life to Christ in that meeting tonight."

Jack took the girls to dinner in his hotel dining room. "I live here but keep hoping to get Holly enthused over a ranch-style home in the suburbs." He winked at Janet.

During dessert a waiter summoned Jack to the phone. As soon as he left, Holly said, "Thanks for staying with me tonight, Jan. It's like I said in my last letter; I can't go on with Jack — unless — but wait! What is that big news you said you'd have, Jan?"

"Greg." Janet's eyes twinkled. Then she explained. "He didn't tell you because he wanted you either to hear it from him personally, or notice it without our telling you. Then when he knew you were coming he said I could tell you because he and Bill had an engagement out of town. They will be back tomorrow."

"Jan! You tease! Now tell me. Hurry, before Jack comes. I can think of two things it might be, and either one is exciting."

"Well, you know Greg has talked many times with us — has asked for help on so many of the Bible questions. He rooms with Bill. In fact, Bill was the one who finally led him to Christ."

"Oh, Jan!" Holly's face glowed. "I'm so happy to hear it. He surely let my folks know?"

"He called them by phone the same day it happened. And when he knew you were coming he decided to wait and surprise you.

"You see, Greg is sure that God is calling him into some kind of full-time service. He thinks it might be evangelistic work. He and Bill are quite close. They have been talking of teaming up — Bill the preacher — Greg the musician — something on that order. We've all three sung together. Bill is a marvelous tenor; I'm really soprano but have to pinch-hit with alto for them. Say, Holly, you sing alto. You'd make the quartet. Greg, of course, is the basso. You should hear us!"

"It sounds great. Yes, that is great news." Holly felt as though she were viewing something attractive but intangible. "Then he isn't going in for the ministry?"

"No. Everyone loves to hear Greg play and sing. He is taking advanced organ lessons, plays at some of the North Street services, and you should hear him give his testimony."

"Will I see him — " Holly began, then paused as Jack crossed the room swiftly. He sat down with an air of elation.

"It's come! The call to leave for Hawaii. Sunday morning at sunrise — jet all the way." His eyes shot sparks. He reached for Holly's hand. "Come with me! Marry me, Holly. You have all day tomorrow to shop and get ready for the trip. Honey, say yes!"

Holly looked down. Why couldn't she respond to such an appeal? Something held her back. She liked Jack the way he was now — the same go-getter he had been in former days when she had wanted to run away with him. After all, she had known him for a long time. Bill was his brother. Surely Bill and she and all of them could win him to Christ in time.

The ranch-style house in the suburbs beckoned. And to think of a honeymoon in blue Hawaii! Liz would swoon at such a proposal. Janet would soon be engaged to Greg and she would be left alone.

What fellowship hath righteousness with unrighteousness? And what communion hath light with darkness? That verse again! Popping into her mind like a bobbin, warning her. Holly knew that God was speaking to her at that moment. *I can't trust Jack completely until he is right with God.*

Her voice sounded far away. "Have you forgotten what you promised?"

He dropped his head. "All right. I promise you I'll think about it, seriously, when I get time. I'm sorry, girls, I can't go with you tonight to church. This call is what I've been waiting for, to give me the big boost with Patterson.

"Some other time I'll go with you — and that is a promise. I'll drop you two off at North Street Church and then dash back to take care of some last minute business. I'll see you tomorrow, Holly, before I leave."

After service that night Holly confided in Janet her desire to know God's will in the matter of love and marriage. When Janet prayed with her, a peace dispelled the confusion and Holly felt relief from sorrow. She retired to the guest rooms where friends and relatives of students were welcome.

It was good to be away from the atheistic atmosphere of State U. As she rested, Holly compared the two schools and decided to enroll in LaSalle the following fall. It was wonderful to be among people who knew God and loved His Word. The warmth of Christian fellowship touched her heart and brought deep comfort which she had missed for a long time.

When she thought of Greg, she could hardly wait to see him and witness the transformation in his life. *If any man be in Christ, he is a new creation . . .*

It was at breakfast that Holly heard the news. Someone in the dining hall said, "Man, did you see the morning headlines? 'Prominent minister, prize-winning author, blackmailed.' Well, what do you know about that? The Reverend Dr. Baines!"

"Janet! Did you hear that?" Holly laid her fork down and half rose from her chair.

"Wait!" warned Janet. "We'll buy a paper outside and take it to my room."

On their way out Holly whispered, "Janet! Does anyone know that Greg is his son?"

"He hasn't mentioned it to anyone except Bill and me — not that I know of, Holly, and you know *we* don't talk."

"I wonder if this is a shock to him or if he knows about it yet. What was it he said in that letter to me? His father would make trouble for him because he quit that other school — the seminary — and came here — except that he was tied up in legal battles with the Strands. Here's the article. I've got to read it, Jan!"

The girls hurried to Janet's room and spread the newspaper on the bed. They both sat down to read.

"Holly," said Janet after they read the first column, "Greg has told me all about Sheila and the way she treated you. He said that by the time you had all reached the Hollister's lodge that day, his eyes were open for the first time to her complete lack of character. This act of revenge shows what type she is, doesn't it? It appears that she has proof of Dr. Baines' treatment of Greg's mother."

"But look here, Janet. He declares that she is deranged and that the letters she possesses are counterfeit. I wonder which one will win the case."

"In the words of the immortal bard, 'the truth will out.' "

"Oh, Janet, I feel so sorry for Greg. Do you suppose he will go straight to his father?"

"He can't go home, Holly. Hasn't he told you? His father was so angry at Greg's decision to change schools, after his big plans for his life, that he told him never to come home again. He had 'humiliated' his father by enrolling in a Bible Institute which teaches that people need salvation. You know he teaches self-righteousness. Greg told us in a prayer group one night that his father had disowned him; since he didn't mention the name of Dr. Baines, I don't think anyone will notice the connection. Let's hope not, for his sake."

"Janet — "

"Yes?"

"Janet, Greg wrote only one letter to me since he first came here in January. I didn't know all this had happened to him. Oh, Janet, don't you just love Greg? He is too good and kind-hearted to receive such cruel treatment."

"Only one letter? All this time? That's unbelievable. He talks about you every time we are together for even a few minutes. Asks me how you are — if I have heard from you — why, what's the matter, Holly?"

Holly buried her face in the papers to hide her emotion. She had forgotten that Greg and Janet were getting closer as friends. No wonder he had not written to her. Janet meant more to him now.

"I've missed him, that's all. It isn't love." Holly sat straight and sniffed. "But, Jan, I just knew he would notice you. You are so perfect for him. You're both in love with music — and all — "

She stammered, sensing that Janet was confused. Holly looked down at the hideous column in the Chicago paper.

Suddenly Janet laughed a little silvery laugh. "Surely you knew it was Bill who interested me. We're engaged, Holly honey. When he can afford a ring, everyone will know, of course. Why, I thought you knew that."

26

Holly looked her surprise. "I didn't have any idea it was you and Bill! Oh, Jan, you'll make a lovely couple in the ministry. It couldn't be better. And Greg is teaming up with you two — "

"That's right. They are talking house trailers these days. In fact, LaSalle may send several of us out as a team to represent the school in churches of many states."

"Jan, that sounds super. Do you know? I decided last night to enroll here next fall."

"Why not make it summer school? We're all staying on. We want to accelerate and get out on the road as soon as possible."

"That's an idea." Holly's eyes glowed with anticipation. "Jan, I'm fed up with the ungodly professors at the university. They are preaching their false religious systems or their atheism and putting their ideas across as truth. I can't sit under it any longer. Besides, I've missed friendship and Christian fellowship and I'm downright homesick. This time with you is a little bit of heaven. I'll hate to go back."

"You'd love the Christian Education course, Holly. It prepares you to help young people or work with children in church. Have you ever thought of putting your talent to work for the Lord? Try some chalk work. Colored chalk — lighting effects — even adults like to see an illustrated Bible story."

Holly thought. "Whatever God wants me to do, I'm ready to do." She knew this included her relationship with Jack Martin. "Janet, my months at this other school were horrible. When I think of the wasted time!"

"Were they worthless?" Janet smiled. "Would you have come to this conclusion about following Jesus all the way — as you told me last night — if you had not seen the other side of the world for yourself? And last but not least, would Greg have been rescued from a completely wasted life? Holly, you should hear him pray. He is like a prodigal son returning to a loving father. He appreciates so deeply the love of God.''

"I know he does," Holly said softly.

"Well, Holly, I have some errands to do for about an hour. Look at my books here until I come back. I have a catalog of LaSalle you can study. Then we can go out to lunch. O.K.?"

Janet was hardly out of the room when Holly heard a knock at the door. A girl smiled and said, "Are you Miss Holly McRae?"

"Yes, I am."

"There is a young man down in the sitting room who wishes to see you."

"Oh, thank you for the message." Holly gathered her coat, purse and boots. Jack would want to drive somewhere. She had better pen a quick note to Janet.

Holly took the elevator down; she found the sitting room crowded with conference visitors and looked around for Jack.

A tall, blond fellow strode across the hall toward her. His big eyes reminded her of someone. She had seen him somewhere — oh, no. It couldn't be. Gwen's boy friend of the ski-lodge party.

"Nels?" she questioned.

"The same." He seemed ill at ease. "I've got to talk to you. Could you get away for a little while? I know a place we can get coffee — "

His hesitation and discomfiture gave Holly reason to believe that he knew of Gwen's trouble and wanted advice from someone. It was natural that he would seek out a pastor's daughter. He probably didn't know a preacher in the whole country.

"I'd love to come," she said kindly.

She followed him to the car lot; he helped her into a sleek blue hardtop of the latest model. He did not talk but threaded through traffic to a freeway where he stepped on the gas.

"Oh, Nels, I should have mentioned that my girl friend expects me back by lunch time."

"It won't take that long," he said. His face was expressionless.

When he drove for ten minutes without trying to exit from the expressway traffic, she felt she must speak.

"Nels, where are we going for coffee? Does it have to be so far?"

He stirred uneasily and spoke from a corner of his mouth. "It's really sort of a practical joke. Remember that girl at the party? Sheila Strand?"

Holly froze. A premonition of danger paralyzed her. She struggled to gain control of herself but couldn't speak without trembling.

"Nels, this is no joke. What does Sheila want with me? You had no business picking me up. I thought you were going to talk to me about Gwen.''

He gave a short laugh. ''Sheila heard you were here in Chi and merely asked me to bring you over for awhile. What's the big deal? Why are you upset? I didn't want to come but she insisted that I get you. Even paid me to make the trip.'' He laughed longer this time.

Holly's thoughts raced in circles. Her father's warning kept flashing red signals but Nel's foot was firm on the gas. She thought of Sheila's brassy look when she faced the wrath of Dr. Baines. She had talked hard and fast to get out of that scrape. *I must think of something to stop him.*

''Nels, I am not going willingly. And if you don't turn around and take me right back, I'll have you charged with kidnapping. You can land in prison for this, you know.''

Nels turned his face and almost veered into the next car. ''Are you kidding? What's so creepy about taking a little ride to see a girl friend? I told you it's only a game. She said she had to see you about something.''

She realized that Nels was unaware of Sheila's strategy.

''Did you read the headlines this morning?'' she cried. ''Well, Sheila threatened Dr. Bruce Baines and he is trying to prove that she is out of her head. She'll want me to testify — oh, you wouldn't know about all this — take me back this instant! Do you hear? There's an exit!''

In her excitement Holly fairly screamed. A sudden fear of the wily girl made her panic.

Nels' ears turned red but he kept driving on the freeway. She recognized the Lake Shore area. It occurred to her that the Strands could afford to pay Nels in four figures — perhaps more. No wonder he would not listen. He had to deliver her over to Sheila in order to collect his handsome reward.

Holly turned her heart to God and breathed a prayer for wisdom. An answering assurance of His presence brought peace. She looked at Nels calmly.

''Your reward in thousands of dollars won't be as valuable to you as keeping out of this court case, Nels.''

He shrugged his shoulders. ''I won't get involved. I'll blow. You can keep this town. It's the open country for me.''

''Yes, that's your speed all right,'' she said contemptuously. ''Just like you 'blew' out on poor Gwen after ruining her whole life. You are a coward and a cheat, and you'll face the judgment of God some — ''

''What did you say?'' Nels shouted suddenly. He wheeled the car in an exit, pulled to a side street and slowed the car.

Holly sensed the fact that Gwen's condition was a complete surprise to him. Perhaps this would help her reason with him.

"Surely you knew about Gwen! She had to leave school because of you. I suppose you didn't even care enough about that lovely girl to keep in touch with her after you made her fall for you." Her cold censure failed to sting him into a reply.

He drove erratically as though he were stunned.

"Gee, Holly. Is it true? I mean — are you sure? She didn't answer my letter. Why didn't she tell me?"

"It is true, Nels. And I could literally beg you to help her. A girl like Gwen is too nice to run out on."

Nels stopped the car. "I didn't run out — I didn't know."

"All right, Nels. Now you know. Will you take me back — or let me out — and then go find Gwen? She is with her aunt."

"Yes. I'll find her. I wanted to marry her but she wasn't ready — "

He grabbed Holly's arm. "No, you don't! Leave that door alone!"

Before Holly could free herself Nels stepped on the gas and the car lurched forward.

"You see, I'm broke. Out of a job. I need that money and something tells me I am being underpaid. I'm delivering you at a certain house; then I'll be free to leave town."

"Nels, it won't matter if you do leave town. The police will find you."

He swerved the car back into traffic and stepped harder on the gas.

27

What more could she do? She had nothing to offer to match Sheila's reward, but she knew God and kept praying. When Nels stopped the car he wouldn't succeed in delivering her to Sheila without a struggle. She would put up a fight.

Nels knew his way. He sped through street canyons lined with apartment buildings as high as cliffs. Soon he pulled into a paved alley and screeched the tires as he careened in a sharp turn. They faced the double doors of an apartment garage. He raced the motor loudly and the doors lifted.

As he stopped the car Nels flashed a small automatic before her face. "Stay! I'll come around and let you out."

Holly stayed. He opened her door and she got out slowly. He took her arm and led her to an elevator. Evidently it was for servants' use. Baggage was stacked on one side. She glanced up at his face. Nels wore a sardonic smirk. He looked self-assured.

They walked down a carpeted hall without meeting anyone. Nels opened and closed a door to a richly furnished apartment.

Sheila stood with her back to a large picture window. She was dressed in slacks and sweater. Holly sensed a change in her manner. She looked hard, but less cocky.

Nels said, "You'd better make it short; she has to get back to a luncheon appointment and I'll take her on my way out."

Sheila took a long draw on her cigarette, her eyes narrowing. "Who is giving orders, friend? You've done your part. My business with Miss McRae is no concern of yours. I'll send her back in a taxi." She handed Nels an envelope.

Holly saw him glance at the contents and noticed the same sarcastic grin widen his lean face. He stood squarely in front of Sheila. "If it's nothing to be ashamed of, go ahead and talk. I choose to wait for her. Good reasons."

Sheila took a step forward and Nels flipped out the little automatic. Sheila laughed and took another step. He gave her a shove with his free hand that made her fall against the window.

She laughed again. "It isn't loaded."

He grinned back. "I took care of that."

Sheila looked sick. A pasty color drained her face of its flushed pink. Holly noticed suddenly that the girl had dark puffs under her eyes. The hand that held the cigarette trembled. Then she turned hard.

"Get out, Nels! I kept my part of the bargain. Now be a gentleman and keep yours."

Nels towered over Sheila with the same grin on his face. "If you were a lady, I'd act like a gentleman. You didn't tell me that you were forcing a person here against her will. Now I demand to know what this is all about. Besides, I'm not the least bit satisfied with the contents of this." He waved the envelope in one hand and the gun in the other.

Sheila sagged against the draperies. "That's all you're going to get. I was only going to appeal to Miss McRae to help me out of a jam. That psychiatrist preacher is so rich and influential that he can afford to hire the best criminal lawyer in the country.

"Holly, you know what a guilt reaction he showed when I told about those personal letters in my possession. My dad has hired lawyers too, but they are having trouble proving my side. The letters were typed and only the signatures were in Lila's and the doctor's handwriting. And Dr. Baines' lawyer is urging him to claim I forged the signatures and framed him. This whole business is about to ruin my father as a publisher instead of punishing the right man." Her face burned red and her voice rose to a high pitch. "I've got to prove what I know for a fact: that Dr. Baines and Lila put Mrs. Baines away because they wanted to get married.

"Holly, you've got to testify as to his reactions that day. You've got to help me prove that doctor's guilt!"

Nels rocked back and forth on both feet as though he were enjoying the scene.

Holly paused to think. Then she said quietly, "You didn't have to threaten the doctor in the first place. I read the morning paper. To beat him to the punch, you tried extortion. He was forced to fight back."

Sheila swore and ground her cigarette out. "I might have known. You'd do anything to help *Greg's father.*" Hatred hardened her eyes.

"No I wouldn't, Sheila. I am not taking either side. I want to stay out of it completely. God is the judge of these things."

"God?" echoed Sheila sarcastically. "Well, you're going to testify or I'll take care of you. Do you understand? Look!" she lowered her voice. "I have one grand in this room. One thousand dollars. It is yours if you'll — "

Nels advanced a step and touched Sheila with the cold automatic. "I suggest you give that to me right now for involving me in a kidnapping case. If you don't hand it over — and quick — I'll testify in court that you paid me to bring this girl to your apartment in order to threaten her. This envelope won't take me far enough. Now get that money fast!"

He nudged her with the gun until she crossed the room to a desk. As she opened a drawer with one hand, she leaned the other arm half-way across the desk.

Holly gasped as she saw Sheila's fingers touch the button.

"Look out, Nels! She rang for help!"

Holly's cry was followed by the sound of doors opening in another room.

Nels' eyes bulged. He threw Sheila aside with one long arm and shouted to Holly. They fled down the hall. The self-service elevator door opened ahead of them. A couple stepped out and Nels pushed Holly inside. He touched the switch for carrying them to the basement.

He panted, "We've got to get my car out. Stay with me."

The elevator glided down slowly.

Perspiration gleamed on Nels' forehead. "We'll be seconds ahead of them. No time to lose. And this gun of Sheila's isn't loaded. I was bluffing."

Slowly the door opened. They bolted for the car.

"My keys!" Nels frantically searched his pockets.

An attendant said, "I'll open the doors, sir. You are in a hurry, I see."

Nels laughed out in relief. "Thanks. Here they are. Run around, Holly."

As he started the motor and Holly ran to the other side, an elevator door opened beside them. Two men yelled, "Hey, you!"

But the hardtop roared and backed into the alley.

A front fender caught Holly and knocked her down. Her head hit a cement post and she blacked out.

Janet read the note Holly left on her desk. "Will try to be back in time for our lunch together but don't worry — you know how Jack is."

By six that evening Janet thought it strange that Holly had not called her. Then she was called to the phone. She heard Jack's voice.

"Holly? Did you ask for Holly?" Janet repeated.

Jack laughed. "Of course. Isn't she there?"

"Jack, I'm worried about her. I was sure she had gone out with you. She left a note for me about eleven this morning. Let me read it to you."

Jack listened and said lightly, "She no doubt met a girl friend and is out having herself a time. Tell you what. You tell her my heart is with her and I'll have to see her when I get back from Hawaii. I wanted to have a quick dinner with her, but won't wait now. The boss needs me tonight. Last minute plans, see?"

"I see." Janet was thinking about Holly but the message filtered through her racing thoughts. "Yes, I'll tell her what you said."

She placed the receiver back dazedly. A premonition of foul play made her shiver. What time this evening were Greg and Bill due to arrive? They might be in now. She rang the boys' dorm.

The house mother said yes, the boys arrived in time for dinner. They had left fifteen minutes ago for the dining room.

Janet raced for the elevator. It never was slower. *Dear God, keep her safe from harm. Help her.*

The dining room was crowded; many guests attending the conference were dining with the students. Janet hurried to Bill's table where he and Greg were conversing with friends. She stood by the wall, her heart beating fast.

Greg looked up first. His eyes widened when he saw her. He nudged Bill. They both rose and she said softly, "Come, please."

She stepped into a corner of the hall and they followed. Swiftly she told them the events of the day.

Greg's face drained of color. He turned to Bill. "You stay close. I may have to call you. I'll go first to my father and question him."

28

Holly awakened to the ring of pain. Her temples throbbed. A cold wet cloth was moving over her face. She tried to move and tensed with pain; her hip felt bruised and ached sharply.

A low voice said, "We didn't plan on this. Now what — "

In a flash Holly was alert. She was in bed. Where? She opened her eyes and looked up at a ceiling. Someone slapped a cold cloth over her eyes. She lunged and snatched the cloth away.

Two young fellows in sweat shirts were hovering over her. Sheila perched on a dressing table. They all looked sober.

"Who are you?" Holly cried out.

The one with the dripping wash cloth and basin said, "Lie down and be quiet. You'll be all right."

The other fellow leered at Sheila and said, "We are her slaves. Speak, Duchess."

"Shut your mouth!" Sheila looked worried. She drew hard on her cigarette.

Holly's pounding head forced her to lie still. The one with the basin piled a second pillow under her shoulders.

"Here's an aspirin." The leering one touched her lips with a tablet.

Holly reacted from intuition. She knocked his hand away and threw the tablet across the room.

"Chee! She's mad!" The leering one leaned over the bed.

"Duke!" Sheila's sharp tone caught him.

"As you say, duchess. You command. We obey. But you'd better think fast. If it was me, I'd say give her a ride into the country."

"It isn't you." Sheila's sarcasm grated like gravel. She coughed and blew smoke.

"I'm not so sure," Duke said silkily. "We weren't counting on this happening."

Holly listened with eyes closed. The slightest move she made caused her head pain. A prayer rose from her heart. *Let Janet know it wasn't Jack.*

"What time is it? I'm getting bored." Duke's whine betrayed a restless spirit.

The one bathing Holly's head answered, "Six."

Holly started to rise but sank back. Her head ached too hard. She must lie still and let the pain recede so she could listen to their conversation. At least she could learn something of their plans.

"Follow that guy Nels?" Duke said under his breath.

Sheila heaved a great sigh. "No use. Let him go. I hope I never see him again."

"Turn on the radio, will you?" whined Duke. "I can't stand it so quiet."

The radio turned in, they listened to "Time for the six o'clock news. World, national, and regional. A special bulletin just received: an unidentified man alerted police this evening that Miss Sheila Strand, of the Dr. Bruce Baines libel case, paid him to pick up a girl she wanted to testify in her behalf. The man, tall, blond, and about twenty-one years of age, claimed innocence in the plot. The police are searching for the missing girl."

Holly looked at the three.

Sheila cried, "Double-crosser!"

The two fellows stared at each other and Duke winked. Then he wheeled and grasped Sheila's wrists. The other one clapped one hand over her mouth while he snatched a scarf from her coat collar. They wound it hard over her mouth and around the back. Duke growled, "Tape's in my pocket. Move!"

The other one snatched the adhesive and bound the girl's wrists and ankles so tightly that she groaned. Without removing the scarf, the fellows taped around her head several times. In their frenzy to be off, they forgot to search her.

Duke unbolted a door and the two fellows ran out.

Holly leaned on one elbow to look at Sheila on the floor. The girl's eyes were blazing and she flopped like a caught fish. Sounds from her throat demanded help.

Holly's one thought was to free the girl from her painful condition. She slid from the bed and sank on her knees beside Sheila. Her head began to throb. Sheila yanked her head toward the dresser, uttering a short and a long subdued squeal which sounded like "in there."

Painfully, Holly opened top drawers and found, among boxes of tape, pills, and a ring of keys, a pair of scissors. She blacked out for a minute and had to lie still.

Sheila pulled herself around and poked Holly with her feet until she came to. Holly looked at her and was alarmed into sensibility.

Sheila's face was purplish red, her eyes glazed and wild.

Holly took the scissors and slashed at the tape on the girl's wrists while her head pounded. She fell back weakly as Sheila yanked free. Only then did she realize what she had done. *She is my enemy. Why did I help her!* She shook from chill.

The girl was out of her head. She grabbed the scissors and cut straight up through the scarf, freeing the adhesive from her mouth. Then she pulled the tape free with one violent yank, tearing hair from her scalp. Without uttering a word she slashed into her taped ankles, blood running as she worked desperately.

When she could stand, Sheila flung on her coat and produced a pistol from her pocket. Holly was too weak and sick to move. She watched the scene as in a bad dream. Sheila stood over her, a sickly smile wavering nervously.

"Your darling doctor is going to pay for this — not me."

"But you — " Holly sank back in a sea of pain. Far away she heard a door open and close.

Greg drove wildly across the city to Lake Shore Drive. He felt an urgency to hurry. Running a caution light that turned red before he got through, he cried out in dismay when a motorcycle zoomed from a side street. In his rear view· mirror Greg spotted the white helmet. The siren wailed and he was forced to pull to the curb.

"O.K., buddy," the officer snarled sarcastically, tipping his helmet back from his face. "Where d'ya think — "

"Reilly!" Greg cried.

"Baines!" The officer gasped. "Say! I read about your father this morning. Are you involved, boy?"

"I can't explain now. Reilly, follow me. My girl disappeared and I'm frantic!"

Reilly took a closer look. "Without wraps in this weather! I reckon you are!"

Greg did not take the garage drive. He pulled into a no-parking gap at the front door of the apartments and leaped out. Reilly roared to a stop behind him.

"God sent you by," Greg panted as they rushed inside.

An elevator opened, people walked out, and the two men pushed the button for their floor. Reilly leaned against the wall and looked at him quizzically.

"Did I hear you right?"

Greg said, "Yes. I found God — or rather, He found me. This girl that's missing started me on the right course." Quickly Greg related the events which led to Holly's disappearance.

As they approached the door to the doctor's apartment, Greg

paused. "We're going to have trouble, one way or another. He told me never to darken his door again."

"Let me darken it," growled Reilly. He marched boldly ahead. No sound met them. Greg pointed to another door. "His study," he whispered. They stepped inside.

"Sheila!"

Greg's exclamation seemed to bring her from a trance. She stood leaning against the wall staring down at the floor.

"I didn't kill him," she said. Then she saw the policeman and screamed, "I didn't do it!"

"We'll see about that." Reilly took two strides and lifted the pistol from her pocket. "And how did you get inside this apartment, young lady?"

Greg knelt by his father.

"Wait!" ordered Reilly. "Hands off." He clanked shiny bracelets on Sheila's wrists. "Cover her while I contact," he barked.

Greg stood guard while Reilly picked up the phone. Sheila began to sob hysterically.

"He was there – on the floor – when I got here."

"Where is Holly McRae?" Greg said evenly.

Sheila's sobs became spasms. She bent over double and Greg caught her arm to steady her.

"Here, sit down. Now tell me what you know."

She seemed irrational. "And I – didn't hurt her – either. No one will believe – "

Reilly stood over her. "It's hard to believe you didn't shoot that man, lady. But it didn't come from this little pistol. Not a cartridge is missing. Let me frisk again." He emptied her purse. "Not a thing," he muttered. "Mighty strange."

He looked hard at Sheila. "O.K. girlie. Tell me your story and don't forget to mention how you got in here."

Greg said quickly, "She has always had keys. Friend of the family."

"I came up – a few minutes ago. He was – here – on the floor." Sheila looked down and screamed. "He's moving!"

"Shut up!" Reilly roared. He went to his knees beside the doctor and felt the man's wrist.

Greg leaned over to look, then strode to Sheila and shook her shoulder. "Tell me about her!"

She clasped her head in her hands. "She's in the Manor Apartments. West side servants' quarters entrance – room three hundred."

"Hold it!" roared Reilly as Greg bolted for the door.

People were gathering in the hall outside. They heard a commotion from the elevators and heavy feet approaching. Two officers flung open the door.

"Ambulance coming," one said briskly. Then the two men proceeded to examine the room.

Greg whispered his fears to Reilly who, in turn, said, "Hold it. We'll be ready to go when this job is over. One thing at a time, boy."

"He's alive but in a coma," they heard from the men.

"Neck and shoulder wounds. Loss of blood."

"This gun?"

"No. Definitely not."

"Then search again."

"Have to leave the rest to the women at headquarters."

Sheila shot across the room for the door. Reilly headed her off, escorted her to a lounging chair and patted her head.

"Whatcha excited about? We'll take care of this. If you weren't the one who did it, we'll find out. Take it easy."

Greg watched the ambulance crew lift his father. His throat grew tight with emotion.

Officers led Sheila away.

"All right, Baines," Reilly rumbled. "Let's go find her."

29

Holly felt the sting of a needle in one arm. She looked at the man in white standing by her bed. He was writing on a tablet. A nurse's cap met her vision on the other side and a cheerful voice told her that it didn't hurt much, did it? She smiled weakly and closed her eyes. The nurse held her wrist.

As the pain in her head lessened, Holly came to life. She felt a sudden nausea. "I'm so hungry," she said. "Nothing to eat all day."

Three voices spoke at once. She heard Greg's exclamation and turned her head to see him. He looked tired but his face glowed with pleasure when she smiled at him. He came near and covered her hand with his big palm.

The nurse beamed. "I'll order two bowls of soup," she said. "Miss McRae, this young man of yours hasn't left your side. He came with you in the ambulance."

"Oh, no!" Holly was shocked. "I'm not that ill. When can I go home?"

The man in white winked at Greg and smiled at her. "You'll be out in a few days. Relax. The doctor will read your x-rays and see you in the morning if not before."

Holly touched her forehead and felt a bandage.

Greg said, "You have a big lump there. Looks like you had been struck a heavy blow." He spoke softly and stroked her hand as though he were speaking to a child.

Holly immediately remembered. She raised her head to sit up but the ache reminded her it was better to rest. "Quick, Greg, find her! Sheila is going to kill your father!"

"It's all right, dear. We found her. Don't think about it any more."

"My head aches. It's so disgusting!" she complained.

"Let me arrange the pillow better." He lifted her shoulder care-

133

fully and poked the pillow into a bigger lump. It was much more comfortable.

Holly thanked him with the glow of her eyes. They understood each other's thoughts and he stood by, waiting.

All at once she realized that it was Greg who had lifted her from the floor in that room. She had come to and heard him say, "Holly, my dearest." Then she was unconscious until the needle pricked her arm.

Looking deeply into his eyes, she knew he cared. At the same instant she knew it was Greg who meant everything to her. The love which overpowered her in that moment was too great for expression. Her eyes filled with tears.

He bent over and whispered, "You are too tired to talk, Holly. Just rest now. I'll be right here."

She heard a chair scrape and knew he was sitting beside her. Again his hand covered hers. The comfort of his presence and warmth of his hand were quieting. She fell asleep.

A bright light overhead and the nurse's clatter woke her.

"You two were sound asleep," she chirped. "But we have some pills to take, and I don't want to go through the red tape again of ordering a lunch after hours. You'd think they had to stop and scrape the carrots and cook the meat to hear them carry on about a simple can of soup. Well, well. Your color is much better, Miss McRae."

As the nurse wheeled her headboard to a higher position, she caught sight of her own face in the dresser mirror.

"Wow!" she said. Her hair stuck out in disarray above and around the ring of gauze. Her face grew pink. "What a sight!"

Greg's eyes smiled into hers through the mirror. "We're happy to see you sitting up and talking like your own cheerful self," he said. Then he held the bowl of soup for her.

It seemed as though he had always been near to help her. There was nothing strange about his presence. Holly marveled at the naturalness of their position. Each time they had been thrown together in strange circumstances, a closer bond had formed between them. *This is love.* She realized that love was a steady glowing comfort which increased in joy as time went by.

A doctor walked in; she recognized the one who had treated her months before. He shook hands with Greg, and said softly, "Better see him for a few minutes; he's awake now. Fifth floor."

She couldn't help asking, "Your father?"

Greg said, "Yes, but he's all right. Promise me you'll rest and not worry about it." He looked soberly into her eyes.

She said quickly, "You'll come back?"

A radiance transformed his face. He seemed overjoyed. Again he drew near and clasped her hand. "I'll be back."

The doctor examined her dressings and said, "You'll be feeling fine in a day or so. The x-rays show nothing to be alarmed about."

"Doctor, please tell me about — the — his father."

"He was admitted to the hospital shortly before you. I'll spend the next few days seeing to both of you." A twinkle of his eyes, a pat on her wrist, and the doctor was gone.

So Sheila had shot him. Greg would tell her about it when he came back. She closed her eyes for a moment and sleep darkened the room.

Someone switched on the overhead light and wakened her from a deep sleep. She wished the nurse would be quiet and leave her alone while she was so comfortable.

"Good morning."

The loud cheerful greeting grated into her consciousness like a dentist's drill.

Holly complained, "What time is it? I'm still asleep."

"Five in the morning!" The nurse's tone seemed to imply that Holly had overslept until noon.

"That young man should have gone home to bed," she told Holly as she jabbed a thermometer into her mouth and took her pulse. "He's slept all night in the sun room at the end of the hall. Wants to see you the minute we'll let him in. Now I'll tell you — I've seen a lot of patients in my day and there aren't many husbands that show so much devotion — let alone fiancees!"

Holly felt the glow from her heart flooding her face. It was good that the nurse had already taken her temperature. "Could he have breakfast in here?" she asked.

"Might as well as to eat it on the cold porch. Now let's try getting up. If you can sit in this chair a minute, I'll make up your bed in a jiffy."

"Oh, glory! My head is a lot better. Just a dull ache. It's not half so sharp." Holly chattered but was glad to lie down again.

She awoke to the sound of rattling dishes in the hall. Her watch read seven-thirty. A girl brought her tray and arranged the bedside table for breakfast.

Greg walked in with a package. He looked tired but his smile was radiant.

Holly sat up on one elbow. "Is that your sack lunch?" she teased.

"Nope." He unwrapped the covering.

She exclaimed in delight. He held a beautiful ornament filled with pink blossoms.

"It's a cyclamen. With best wishes and love from Janet, Bill and

135

me. By the way, Holly, your folks will be here to see you shortly. They drove into the city late last night when they heard about you. You'll have a crowd in here this afternoon, too, because Janet and Bill want to come. So I thought — I'd say hello now — " he hesitated, arranged the plant on the dresser and walked slowly back. Then, helping her with the coffee cream, he went on. "I'll leave for church. You won't have room for me after they come."

"Yes, I will, Greg. But you really should get some rest. The nurse told me you stayed out in the cold sun porch all night. You might catch cold."

Greg stood near but did not come closer as he had the night before. "Don't you have a tray! They'll give you one," she said.

"I can eat in the cafeteria at eight."

There was a moment of silence as she bowed her head. Suddenly she remembered what Janet had told her. "Greg, the news that I heard is the most wonderful news in the world. I'm so glad you've met the Lord as your own Saviour and Friend."

"It is exactly as the Book says," Greg said eagerly. He took a New Testament from his pocket. "'If any man be in Christ, he is a new creature' — 'a new creation' — and 'old things are passed away; behold, all things are become new.' Holly, I can't describe the peace in my heart and the deep joy Jesus gives. I have just begun to live."

They both turned to see who was coming. Holly's mother came quickly across the room followed by Pastor McRae and Janet Eagan.

Everyone talked at once. Janet brought a small radio and Greg found a place for it by Holly's bed.

After the greetings, Holly's father said, "Greg, did you see the Extra edition of the news this morning?"

"No, sir. I haven't been outside the hospital. What was it?"

Pastor McRae motioned them all closer and lowered his voice. "The mystery of the shooting has been solved. When Sheila's father heard that she was 'suspect,' he confessed that he was the one. Said he had gone to the doctor's apartment to try reasoning with him, and the doctor was — as he put it — utterly unreasonable. He said that after he was threatened, he lost his head and shot the man."

"But he was carrying a gun, wasn't he?" said Greg. "Wouldn't that prove it was premeditated?"

"He claimed that he carried it for protection, knowing the doctor's temper. And the police found a loaded revolver in the doctor's desk drawer. So each man was prepared for something more than mere verbal battle. How is he, Greg? Will we have an opportunity to speak to him?"

"I want you to tell him about Christ," Greg said. "He won't listen to me. Shall we go now? I must hurry to the dorm and change before church. Have to play the organ, you know."

"We'll be back in a few minutes." Holly's father kissed her cheek and left with Greg.

Mrs. McRae listened to Holly's experiences and Janet's part in the drama. When Holly told of Greg's night watch, she added shyly, "Mother — Janet — I believe I'm beginning to discover what real love is. I care so much about Greg that — that it hurts deep inside. I just discovered it last night while he was here. He was so kind and understanding — and I miss him more each time he goes away. I've never missed Jack except for the excitement he created. With Greg — Janet, you know what I mean."

"Yes, I know. There are no doubts in your mind as there were concerning your friendship with Jack. Isn't that it?"

"Exactly."

Her mother said, "Honey, do you know what he told us some time ago when he came to Dayton? He came several times for spiritual counsel and once he confided in us; he told us how much he cared for you. But he was extremely hopeless because of something you said on that last trip with him from Chicago. You gave him the impression that you would never consider marrying the type of man he is — or was —"

"What did I say?" Holly cried. "I can't remember. But I didn't mean to give him any such idea."

Janet smiled. "God will work it out. 'Wait on the Lord.' Hush! Here they come."

30

The two men were talking together as they came in; both looked sad.

Greg saw the question on their faces and told them, "My father wasn't sorry to see us but he wasn't happy about it either. Raved about the Strands and what he'd do to them when he gets on his feet."

Holly's father said, "He did go so far as to admit he has made some sad 'mistakes' in his day."

"Yes," said Greg bitterly. "He doesn't admit there is such a bad thing as sin." Then he brightened. "Holly, your father prayed for my father. Was I ever thrilled! You should have heard his prayer. I was so overcome with the knowledge of my father's lost condition that I added one of my own. And you should have seen his face."

"He was too ill to remonstrate," smiled the pastor. "We'll pray that something will touch his heart. He has hardened himself against God for so long.

"Well, Holly girl, we'll go along and let you rest. After church we'll be back to cheer your day. My, how we praise the Lord for keeping you. He has surely watched over you, honey."

Greg looked for a long moment into her eyes. Holly's response brought him to her side. He clasped her hand and she said quietly, "Please come back. If not early, late afternoon?"

His soul looked through his eyes and she read the desire of his heart. Again she felt the tightening of the bond between them.

Janet said, "Let me stay with her. We'll listen to North Street Church over the radio. And when she wants to sleep I'll read. I don't like to leave her here alone today. It was so terrifying to lose her yesterday."

Knowing Janet's loyalty to her church, they were all surprised at this speech.

"You will miss your Sunday school class," said Holly.

"They'll go double with another class today. It won't create too much havoc," Janet declared.

"I think it is lovely and thoughtful of you," said Mrs. McRae, kissing her and Holly good-by.

As they left, the doctor entered, followed by an intern and a nurse. Holly recognized the man in white of the night before.

"Good news this morning," the doctor announced. "Your condition is quite satisfactory and you may go home tomorrow — "

Janet and Holly exclaimed in delight.

"If — " he continued, "you will rest for a few days. And no school for two weeks."

"Won't this be a surprise to your folks?" Janet said, when they were alone.

"Yes," said Holly. "They can attend the conference tonight and take me to Dayton with them tomorrow. Oh — "

Her face clouded and Janet began to tease.

"He'll be coming to see you. Don't worry."

"How do you know?"

"Sixth sense."

A nurse brought medicine for Holly and Janet prepared to read.

"Do wake me for the eleven o'clock service," Holly reminded her. "I want to hear Greg playing the organ."

The hours she slept seemed as minutes. When Janet tuned in to the North Street Church, Holly was refreshed and ready to listen.

It was good to hear the familiar hymns and gospel songs.

Janet said, "Greg's morning mood is more in keeping with the worship service. You'll just have to hear him some Sunday night when he lets out all the stops and zips up and down the keyboard. I wouldn't miss a Sunday night service for the world. The music lifts us out of our seats."

"I can imagine." Holly curled up and leaned her head on the pillow. "I'm so glad you stayed with me, Jan. It seems more like church."

"Let's pray for Greg's father and for Sheila and her family." Janet bowed her head.

While the church announcements were being aired, the girls had prayer together. Then the speaker caught their attention with the words, "All things work together for the benefit of those who love the Lord, that they might be conformed to the image of Christ."

The girls listened intently to the message from the eighth chapter of Romans. Knowing that Greg was receiving the same encouraging words gave them a thrill.

At twelve noon the North Street Church service was cut off and the announcer droned: "Time for the twelve o'clock news." Janet was about to switch the dial but decided to listen. "A western Air Lines DC jetliner bound for Hawaii via Los Angeles with fifty-eight

139

persons aboard crashed and burned today, minutes after takeoff from Los Angeles.

"Officials reported no survivors.

"Those aboard included three businessmen from Chicago: Dr. Howard Green, James Milland, and Jack Martin."

The girls stared at the radio, then at each other, trying to absorb the shock. It was impossible! Someone so alive as Jack. Eating with them only yesterday it seemed — exuberant in the prospects of a brilliant future — gay — nonchalant.

The awful truth stunned Holly. His words returned from the abyss which separated them. *"Why didn't you talk like this a long time ago? It might have helped — then. I liked to hear your father preach but I thought you weren't 'sold' on all this . . . "*

Too late. Eternity. Too late. Eternity. Lost. Forever lost. The words shot through her brain in flaming neon signs. She was too late to win Jack to Christ. Her head began to throb.

Janet flipped off the radio. "You must not worry, Holly. Remember the message we heard? And God kept me here on purpose that you wouldn't get this news alone. I had the strongest feeling this morning that I should stay here. Now I know why."

"Turn it on, Janet. Maybe we'll hear more. I'm all right."

Janet turned to another station that was also carrying the story.

"The huge plane, 126 feet long, had one stop scheduled for Los Angeles. Western officials said that twenty-three persons boarded the flight in Chicago and another thirty-three at L.A. The plane was air-borne. At 8:17 its 'blip' vanished from control tower radar screens. Captain Roth was on course when the plane crashed . . . "

Janet flipped the dial. "It's too horrible," she cried. "Jack was on *his* course when that plane crashed — his self-centered course which put God in the background until a more convenient time to meet Him. Doesn't it make God's Word fairly shout, 'Now is the day of salvation . . . what will it profit a man, if he shall gain the whole world, and lose his own soul?' "

"He followed me." Holly stared ahead. "If I had been following the Lord in those days at high school, Jack might have followed Him too."

Janet stood by, unable to help. She prayed silently. It was a relief to see the McRaes walk in. They had received the news on their car radio. It was good to hear the pastor's kind words.

He held his daughter's hands. "We know how you feel, honey. But Jack did hear the Gospel many times; you did bring him to church. He knew you were a Christian. And one time when he was waiting for you in the living room I talked with him about salvation in Christ and urged him not to put off this greatest decision in life. I told him then: 'the tragedy of all tragedies is the soul that goes into eternity without the righteousness of Christ for a covering.' I told him that he couldn't stand before God in his rags of self-righteousness."

"Dad — Mother — I'll never forget how I failed to live for the Lord in those days. This will be a constant reminder to me. I'm giving my life to Jesus Christ and asking Him to use me from now on for His honor and glory. And I want to change schools. Janet suggested summer school at LaSalle. What do you think of that?"

It seemed they all talked at once, each one interested in her plans. When her tray arrived, Holly remembered their needs.

"Now you all go out to dinner. Take Janet or she'll waste away here, watching me enjoy this turkey and dressing."

"We forgot to tell them the good news!" Janet looked at Holly.

"Oh, yes, folks. I can go home with you tomorrow. How about that?"

"That's another prayer answered," her father said gravely. Then he bent to kiss her.

"I should stay here." Mrs. McRae hesitated at the door.

"I'd better take a nap, Moms. Go ahead and enjoy eating out for a change. You hardly ever get to eat a Sunday dinner you haven't worked hard to prepare."

Her mother smiled. "You be sure and rest then," she said.

Holly rested and fell into light slumber. The knowledge of Jack's sudden death pierced through. She awakened with tears running down her face.

A warm hand covered hers and Greg whispered, "Did he mean so much to you, Holly?"

She clasped his hand and cried, "It isn't that, Greg. I didn't care — like that. It's just that — that I was not living the way I should when he started dating me in high school. I wish I had those days to live over."

Suddenly she felt his arm around her. His face touched hers and he whispered, "We both know what it means to walk apart from God; you haven't fallen as I have, but the sting is there. I know how you feel, dearest. Holly, do you think you could ever forget my past — and —"

He stopped short. Bill's voice came distinctly from the hall; then he walked in with Janet, followed by the McRaes.

Holly smiled at Greg through her tears.

31

While they were assembled in Holly's room a nurse came in asking for "Mr. Baines."

"Doctor wants to see you on fifth floor," she said.

Greg looked at Pastor McRae.

Holly's father said quickly, "Do you need me? All right, son. I'll be back shortly, folks."

Bill turned to Mrs. McRae. "I am driving home after we leave the hospital. I phoned my mother that I'd be there tonight. I hope she decides to ask Pastor to take the service. But in case she has already contacted that modernistic preacher in town—I know you will understand it wasn't my wish."

"Of course, Bill. Be careful on the road, won't you?"

"Don't worry. I hope we'll hear about Greg's father before I leave."

Bill and Janet took chairs and talked together while Holly and her mother visited.

Soon the pastor came in. He went to Holly's side and they all gathered around to hear. He took a handkerchief from his pocket and wiped his face.

"It looks as though Greg's father is in for some years of intense mental suffering. The doctor just told us that the result of Dr. Baines' neck injury is a sudden paralysis of the right side of his body. He knows what is going on and can talk but is terrified, naturally. He has no one bigger than himself to trust.

"Now I know what the words compassion and pity mean. You can't help but feel sorry for him."

Mrs. McRae said slowly, "What a man sows, that shall he also reap. God's Word does not lie."

"We must pray much for Greg in this trial," Bill said. "Holly, you have meant more to him than you perhaps realize. He broke down and wept the night he was saved, mainly because of his wasted years.

"He said that because of his alliance with Sheila, he was afraid he didn't have a chance with you. He thinks so highly of you that — as he told me — 'She's so far above me, I'll never be able to face her. She's like an angel in my life.' It was your life, Holly, that was a most effective testimony to Greg. He had never before met a girl like you."

Holly sighed. "If only it had been that way — with your brother."

"'God is greater than our heart and knoweth all things,'" Bill quoted the familiar Scripture and looked at his watch. "Is Greg coming down?"

Pastor McRae said, "Probably not. He phoned the church for a substitute musician tonight and said to tell you folk about it."

"Then I'll say good-by. Must get on the road. Are you taking Janet to church with you, or shall I drop her off?"

"We'd better stay here, Bill. Greg might need us. We'll likely be home by late afternoon, in case you need us there. Take it easy now. We'll be praying for you as you travel."

After Janet and Bill left, the doctor came in to see Holly.

"Glad to meet this girl's family," he said cordially. "Yes, you may take her home in the morning. Greg's father. Sad case. Looks like the end of the legal battles between him and the Strands. Both families will continue to suffer for — God knows how long. The doctor's business is finished; scandal slays a minister, as you well know, Pastor.

"Well, young lady, no more broken bones or knocking yourself out like this. Watch your step from now on."

"I shall," she said, mentally adding, *in more ways than one.*

Later in the evening Greg hurried in. He said quickly, "I'll have to see to things for father. Papers in his study and at the bank. They are transferring him to another hospital. So — I'll have to go. Take a day or so from school — but can't be helped."

"We'll be holding you up before the Lord. He will give you strength for each day." Pastor McRae shook hands.

Greg went to Holly.

For a time they were speechless. Then she said, "Come down to see us as soon as you can get away."

Mother McRae echoed her words. Greg pressed their hands and was gone.

On the way home next day her father told Holly, "The doctor would have kept you longer but he didn't want to take any more chances with Sheila. The way she threatened you alerted the police.

"Janet related the account you gave her to Greg's friend, Reilly, who was on the case."

"I'm not afraid of her trying any more stunts," said Holly. "She's

143

had it, I'd say. She won't be looking for me, now that the doctor is unable to fight it out in a trial."

"You are right," said her mother. "And in all this, Greg hasn't been forced to witness against his own father. That publicity would have been hard on him."

"I love that boy." Holly's father glanced at her through the rear-view mirror. "All his pompous oratory and pride are gone. He is a new creature in Christ Jesus. It has been a thrill to see him grow in grace.

"You know, Holly, his father's behavior humiliated him. That, along with Sheila's tirades caused him to think you would despise him. But by the looks of things — "

Holly, reclining in the back seat, laughed aloud. Her mother turned around and winked at her.

It was good to get home. The same evening Greg called from Chicago.

"Just to hear you say you're all right," he explained to Holly. "May I come down next weekend? Bill called to say that his mother is completely broken up over Jack's — over the tragedy. He thinks that he can get her out to church Sunday. So we're all three coming down. Janet says she'll drop everything to be with Bill."

"Wonderful. You don't need to ask if you can come, Greg — ever. I miss you." She dropped her voice shyly but he heard.

"I love you, Holly."

The tremble in his quick utterance thrilled her. She caught her breath and found her own heart beating wildly as she tried to keep her voice steady.

"I love you."

"Holly, I can't wait to see you."

"The week will be an eternity."

"You know I'd get away tonight — I'd come now — if it were possible."

"I know you would. But you must take care of things there first. Then you will be free to enjoy the time here?"

"You bet I will. Holly, you are — my dearest one." He held the last words carefully, that she would hear and know.

Holly placed the receiver in a whirl of ecstasy. She leaned her head on her arm and let the full glory of his love fill her to overflowing.

That week was a century long. Each morning she counted the days until Friday. On Friday she felt well enough to go on a short shopping expedition. When she returned, her father said that Greg had called. He and Bill were unable to make the trip until late Saturday night. Janet would be with them and they would see Holly Sunday at church.

"I asked Greg to play the organ and Janet the piano."

"Good. You think of everything, Dad. Could you ask Bill to at least give a testimony? It might help win his mother."

"*You* think of everything," he echoed.

Holly drifted through the next day in a dream world. Jo Ann and Timmy grew exasperated at her absent-minded answers to their many questions.

"I'll be glad when he gets here!" Timmy declared. "Then maybe you'll wake up."

Holly was wide awake Sunday morning. She sat beside her friend, Carol, in the back of the church and watched breathlessly as Greg and Janet took their places by the platform.

Greg nodded at Janet and they began to play.

"Simply super!" Carol whispered. "They say this young Baines used to be a whizz in night clubs. Oh, I forgot. You have met him, haven't you?"

"Yes." Holly smiled.

They stood to sing and she saw Greg turn his head and glance around the church. She felt her face scorch when their eyes met. The light that broke across his face was beautiful; his smile erased the shade of sorrow, and sunshine flooded her soul.

The special music with Greg's organ background for vocalists prepared their hearts for Bill's stirring testimony.

Carol nudged Holly. "Look, down front, center aisle. Isn't that Mrs. Martin, Jack and Bill's mother?"

"It is!" breathed Holly.

She was thrilled to hear her father's message. It couldn't be plainer. An invitation was extended to accept the greatest offer ever made: the gift of eternal life through Christ Jesus.

They rose to sing "Just As I Am." One young man responded to the invitation. Holly was thrilled to see Bill's mother, in her mink stole, step out from her seat. A sob escaped the woman's lips as she went forward to meet the pastor. Bill clasped her in his arms and Janet left the piano to stand by her side.

"How perfectly wonderful!" Carol rejoiced. Then she added soberly, "But what it takes, sometimes, to bring someone to the Lord."

Holly met Greg at the organ. He said huskily, "My car is outside. Let me drive you home."

They parked in McRae's driveway and he drew her close. "I loved you so much that I didn't dare write for fear I would say something that would be the wrong thing. I am so utterly unworthy. I was sure you were despising me because of my past life — "

She cried, "I despise myself. I am most unworthy of God's love."

They remained silent for a moment, understanding each other's thoughts. Quietly, he held her hand and placed a ring on her finger.

The triple diamond sparkled in a heart shape.

"It was my mother's," he whispered. "Her initials are inside. I found it in a safety box at the bank, so — it is new to me too."

She lifted her face to his and the kiss was at least a minute long. Timmy's exclamation from outside the car brought them back.

"Great jumpin' — " he said, his face turning red.

Holly opened her door and Greg said, "That's O.K., Timmy. Get in a minute. How would you like to attend a wedding this summer?"

"Yours?" Timmy looked at Greg, embarrassed.

"Why not?" Holly said, hugging him.

"Boy! What a rock!" Timmy lifted her hand and the gem sent colored lights into their eyes. Then he jumped from the car and spun into the house to announce the good news.

"Holly, you're wanted on the phone," Jo Ann called. "Hurry! Long distance!"

Holly lifted the receiver and Liz's strong voice came through.

"Hol, guess where I am! At Gwen's wedding. Are they ever the most handsome, happy couple. Nels just arrived yesterday and he's too nervous to talk but she makes up for that.

"What have you been up to? You're *what?* Engaged? Well, it's about time you got some sense. Lucky kid! I fell for that Jack Martin but he didn't give me a break — and believe me, I gave him a good chase!"

"Liz, listen! It wasn't — "

"Gotta go, Hol. I'll tell the gang and we'll all shower you too. Congratulations to that handsome man! Give him my love — "

"Liz, wait!"

A click was the only answer.